WHEN THE CAT'S AWAY

A COMEDY IN TWO ACTS

BY

JOHNNIE MORTIMER & BRIAN COOKE

SAMUEL FRENCH, INC.
45 WEST 25TH STREET   NEW YORK 10010
7623 SUNSET BOULEVARD   HOLLYWOOD 90046
LONDON   *TORONTO*

Copyright © 1989 by Johnnie Mortimer and Brian Cooke

ALL RIGHTS RESERVED

CAUTION: Professionals and amateurs are hereby warned that WHEN THE CAT'S AWAY is subject to a royalty. It is fully protected under the copyright laws of the United States of America, the British Commonwealth, including Canada, and all other countries of the Copyright Union. All rights, including professional, amateur, motion pictures, recitation, lecturing, public reading, radio broadcasting, television, and the rights of translation into foreign languages are strictly reserved. In its present form the play is dedicated to the reading public only.

The amateur live stage performance rights to WHEN THE CAT'S AWAY are controlled exclusively by Samuel French, Inc., and royalty arrangements and licenses must be secured well in advance of presentation. PLEASE NOTE that amateur royalty fees are set upon application in accordance with your producing circumstances. When applying for a royalty quotation and license please give us the number of performances intended, dates of production, your seating capacity and admission fee. Royalties are payable one week before the opening performance of the play to Samuel French, Inc., at 45 West 25th Street, New York, NY 10010-2751; or at 7623 Sunset Blvd., Hollywood, CA 90046-2795, or to Samuel French (Canada), Ltd., 100 Lombard Street, Toronto, Ontario, Canada M5C 1M3.

Royalty of the required amount must be paid whether the play is presented for charity or gain and whether or not admission is charged.

Stock royalty quoted on application to Samuel French, Inc.

For all other rights than those stipulated above, apply to Peters, Fraser and Dunlop, 503/4 Chambers, Chelsea Harbor, London SW10 OXF, England.

Particular emphasis is laid on the question of amateur or professional readings, permission and terms for which must be secured in writing from Samuel French, Inc.

Copying from this book in whole or in part is strictly forbidden by law, and the right of performance is not transferable.

Whenever the play is produced the following notice must appear on all programs, printing and advertising for the play: "Produced by special arrangement with Samuel French, Inc."

Due authorship credit must be given on all programs, printing and advertising for the play.

ISBN 0 573 69131 2   Printed in U.S.A.

Anyone presenting the play shall not commit or authorize any act or omission by which the copyright of the play or the right to copyright same may be impaired.

No changes shall be made in the play for the purpose of your production.

The publication of this play does not imply that it is necessarily available for performance by amateurs or professionals. Amateurs and professionals considering a production are strongly advised in their own interests to apply to Samuel French, Inc., for consent before starting rehearsals, advertising, or booking a theatre or hall.

No part of this book may be reproduced, stored in a retrieval system, or transmitted in any form, by any means, including mechanical, electronic, photocopying, recording, videotaping, or otherwise, without the prior written permission of the publisher.

IMPORTANT BILLING AND CREDIT REQUIREMENTS

All producers of WHEN THE CAT'S AWAY *must* give credit to the Authors of the Play in all programs distributed in connection with performances of the Play and in all instances in which the title of the Play appears for purposes of advertising, publicizing or otherwise exploiting the Play and/or a production. The name of the Authors *must* also appear on a separate line, in which no other name appears, immediately following the title, and *must* appear in size of type not less than fifty percent the size of the title type.

The first performance of WHEN THE CAT'S AWAY was held in June 1977, at the Pier Theatre, Bournemouth, with the following cast:

MILDRED ROPER....................Yootha Joyce
GEORGE ROPER...................Brian Murphy
ETHEL POMFREY.....................Dilys Laye
HUMPHREY POMFREY.......Reginald Marsh
JENNIFER FRAZER.................... Sue Bond
SHIRLEY.......................Roseanne Wickes

CAST

MILDRED ROPER
GEORGE ROPER
ETHEL POMFREY
HUMPHREY POMFREY
JENNIFER FRAZER
SHIRLEY

TIME

THE PRESENT

PLACE

THE ROPER'S HOUSE IN HAMPTON WICK

ACT I

Scene 1	Saturday, 3:30 pm
Scene 2	Saturday, 9:00 am (One week later)

ACT II

Scene 1	Saturday, 12 midnight
Scene 2	Sunday, 9 am

EPILOGUE

ACT I

Scene 1

TIME: The present. About 3:30 on a Saturday afternoon in summer.

SCENE: The living room of a house in Hampton Wick, the home of George and Mildred Roper. It's a modern house, built for the young executive market, but the furniture lets it down, a bit too old, a bit too cheap and a bit too vulgar. A reproduction of "The Green Lady" hangs on the wall and sets the tone for the room
It is a split level and stairs lead up UL to a raised landing running UL to UR, which has doors leading off to the bedroom and the bathroom. The equivalent of the first floor if this were not a dormer bungalow. At the UR end of the landing is a small table, containing a large plant, which partly obscures the face of a grandmother clock behind it.
From the DS living area there is a door DR which leads to the kitchen. Next to it is a partly open hatch. DL there is a row of coat pegs, with several coats hanging on them, the front door,

7

a window beside it and next to that, at right angles, a door to the downstairs W.C. and cloakroom. these lead off from a slightly raised area, divided off by a rail or low room divider to give the feel of a small entrance hall. One step leads down into the main living area. Next to the front door DS, is a table with a telephone on it.

Underneath the hatch DR is a gate-leg dining table, now folded and stacked against the wall. Four dining chairs next to it, two either side.

DCL is a convertible settee, set at a slight angle, but mainly facing DS. Beside it is a matching armchair and in front a low coffee table. On the table are some holiday brochures, and an ashtray.

DL is a TV set. UC beneath the raised landing is a long sideboard containing some tasteless ornaments, a bottle of wine, a soda syphon and a piggy bank .A table lamp, a record player and some records.

AT RISE: GEORGE backs in from the kitchen. He's sloppily dressed in a baggy cardigan, slippers, etc. He carries a tray of condiments, cutlery, bottle of brown sauce. He's talking back into the kitchen as he enters. He's defiant.

GEORGE. No, no, no, no, no! I'm sorry, Mildred. My mind is made up. I am not going. I will not hear another word! (*He dumps the tray on the gate-leg table and wags a finger through the hatch.*) And it's no use you foldin' your arms and tightenin' your lips! (*Moves down center and declaims.*) It's pointless discussin' the matter further! D'you understand, Mildred?

MILDRED. (*Lets herself in the front door. She's wearing a coat and carries a shopping bag containing groceries.*) George?

GEORGE. (*Startled.*) Nyaa ... (*He falls over the chair.*)

MILDRED. Who were you shouting at? I could hear you in the street.

GEORGE. I was ... I was talking to myself.

MILDRED. At the top of your voice? (*She hangs her coat on the coat pegs.*)

GEORGE. Ah, well ... I ... my hearing's not what it was, Mildred.

MILDRED. Mmmm. Just make sure you never speak to *me* in that tone of voice.

GEORGE. Oh, I wouldn't, my sweet. I'm ... I was just about to set the table. (*During the following, he pulls the gate-leg table out from the wall and sets it up. He places the four dining chairs around it.*)

MILDRED. Good ... (*A thought, she delves in her shopping bag.*) Oh, I've got a new set of place mats ... (*Produces a cellophane wrapped set of four medium place mats, plus a large one.*) "The

Royal Children," coated in heat-resistant melamine. So tasteful.

GEORGE. I don't want that lot gawpin' up at me while I'm havin' me dinner! What's wrong with our "Festival o' Britain" set?

MILDRED. They are old and they are warped.

GEORGE. I like 'em.

MILDRED. You would! (*Slaps place mats into his hands.*) Lay them out! Respectfully! (*She exits to the kitchen with her shopping bag. He rips the cellophane from the place mats, grumbling.*)

GEORGE. It's ridiculous. I bet you *he* hasn't got *our* pictures on *his* place mats. (*Taps mat.*) Probably got "The Goons," or someone like that ...

(*MILDRED comes from the kitchen, carrying sideplates and a bowl of salad. She places them on the table and crosses to the sideboard.*)

MILDRED. By the way, while I was out, I called in on the travel agent ... I've got our tickets!

GEORGE. Ah! ... (*Stiffens, clears throat. The moment for which he's been preparing!*) No, no, no, no. I'm sorry, Mildred. My mind is made up. I'm not going. I will not hear another word! (*She turns, folds her arms and looks tightlipped. He has his back to her.*) And it's not use your foldin' your arms and tightenin' your lips!

MILDRED. (*She looks slightly surprised, since he can't see her.*) It's pointless discussing the matter further, George.

GEORGE. (*Still quoting himself.*) It's pointless discussing ... Eh?

MILDRED. We're going! I've booked!

GEORGE. I don't want to go on holiday, Mildred ... Not abroad!

MILDRED. It's not a holiday! It's a second honeymoon!

GEORGE. What was wrong with the first?

MILDRED. (*She stares at him in disbelief for a long moment, then raises her left index finger as though to start counting off a long list. Takes a deep breath, the words fail her.*) Everything!

GEORGE. Mildred ... that was twenty-five years ago ... you've been holding it against me ever since. What I mean is, at the time, I was ... young and inexperienced. And now, I'm ... well ...

MILDRED. Old and inexperienced. (*She comes over to the table with napkins and four wine glasses.*)

GEORGE. No! I grant you I was perhaps a little over-eager ...

MILDRED. Oho, that's a new one. It's taken you twenty-five years to think that one up! (*Thrusts napkins at him.*) Lay 'em out!

GEORGE. Serviettes?

MILDRED. Napkins! All I'm saying, George, is that I am approaching middle age ...

(*She sits on the settee, looking wistfully at travel brochures.*)

GEORGE. From which direction?

MILDRED. No, I must face up to it ... and I thought it would be nice to ... recapture some of the magic and romance ... that weren't there in the first place.

(*He crosses to behind the settee, realizing that she's a bit emotional, not sure what to do about it.*)

MILDRED. The same little town in France ... the same small hotel ... same bedroom ...

GEORGE. Yes, but you're overlookin' one thing, Mildred. It'll be the same you an' me.

MILDRED. We can try, George. All it needs is a little sympathy, a little understanding of each other's needs ... love ...

GEORGE. (*Musing.*) Same town ...? Same hotel ...? Same bedroom ... um ... I s'pose it could work ... except for one thing.

MILDRED. What?

GEORGE. (*Moving to table again.*) I'm not goin'!

MILDRED. (*Hate.*) Ooh ...!

GEORGE. I don't like flying! It's unnatural for a man to go hurtling through the air at five hundred miles an hour!

MILDRED. (*Stands.*) It may be unnatural, but it's going to happen at any moment!

GEORGE. (*Backs away from her 'round the table.*) Now, now, Mildred ... not in front o' the Royal children. Can't you ... can't you go on your own?

MILDRED. What sort of second honeymoon would that be? (*Answers herself.*) Exactly the same as the first! Come here ...

GEORGE. No, no ... look, they'll be arrivin' soon. You don't want 'em to find us squabbling.

MILDRED. What? (*Checks her wristwatch, calms down.*) Ah ... (*Instantly brisk.*) Get the floral centerpiece ... and take that brown sauce with you ... cushions, cushions ... (*Starts to tidy up, plumping cushions, etc.*) You haven't heard the last of this, George ... and open the bottle of wine.

GEORGE. (*Exits to kitchen, with brown sauce.*) All right, all right.

MILDRED. I want everything to be just so. You know what my sister's like. When it comes to dust, she's got a finger like a laser beam!

(*GEORGE comes from the kitchen with a floral centerpiece, which he plonks on the table. Mumbles darkly.*)

MILDRED. What was that?
GEORGE. I said, "She's a flippin' nuisance!"
MILDRED. Aha! (*Picks up the piggy bank.*) Swearbox!
GEORGE. "Flippin'" isn't swearing!

MILDRED. It *is!*
GEORGE. It bloody isn't!
MILDRED. That is! (*Rattles it at him.*) Swearbox!

(*He dips in his pocket and puts a coin in the box. this is obviously a well established routine.*)

GEORGE. Gor blimey ... (*Mumbles darkly.*)
MILDRED. You're mumbling!

(*GEORGE picks up a bottle of wine which is standing on the sideboard. There is already a pull type corkscrew in the cork.*)

GEORGE. Look here, Mildred, I'll make no bones about it ... (*He struggles to pull the cork, without success.*) ... umph. I do not like your Ethel ... and I do not like her husband, Humpty Dumpty.
MILDRED. Humphrey Pomfrey. (*She crosses to the window by the front door and looks out.*)
GEORGE. Yes, him! The offal king of Oxshott. Just 'cos he's got a bit o' money ... (*Continues to struggle with cork.*) ... umph ... he thinks he's better than me. And ... umph ... *she* thinks he's better than me ...
MILDRED. Three votes to one! Motion carried!
GEORGE. If you're that fond of him, take 'im on your second honeymoon ... umph ...

MILDRED. At least he's a *man*.

GEORGE. (*Crossing to her. Offended dignity.*) I see. Are you implyin' that I am not?

MILDRED. I didn't *say* that ...(*She takes the bottle of wine from him and plucks the cork from it without any effort. Hands it back to him. He looks at it, crosses to the table with it, then ...*)

GEORGE. (*Defensive.*) Yes, well ... I'd loosened it, hadn't I.

MILDRED. Just put it on the ... (*Sees something out of window.*) There's a taxi, George! It'll be them! And you're not even changed!

GEORGE. What's wrong with me as I am?

MILDRED. Just *look* at yourself! All we need is the tin man and the cowardly lion! Get changed!

GEORGE. (*Starts up stairs.*) Oh, all right ... if it's gonna be lah-di-dah time. What shall I wear? (*Attempts Noel Coward accent.*) The velvet smoking jacket? Goes with the top 'at and the ivory fag-holder. (*Sings.*) "Some day I'll find you ... "

MILDRED. Get up there!

(*He scurries into the bedroom as the front doorbell rings. MILDRED straightens her hair, etc., switches on a smile and opens the front door. She admits ETHEL, her sister. ETHEL wears a fur coat and is expensively dressed, though without taste. She's under some strain, but hiding it.*)

MILDRED. Ethel, darling, how lovely to see you ... (*A kiss.*) And Humphrey ... (*Turns to greet HUMPHREY at door, realizes he isn't there.*) ... er ... where's Humphrey?

ETHEL. He's not coming, Mildred. Oh, what a sweet little dress. You *must* let me have the paper pattern!

MILDRED. What?

ETHEL. For my au pair. Consuela loves bright colors. Will you give me a hand with my suitcases, darling?

MILDRED. Yes, of course. I ... (*She brings the expensive suitcases from the front doorstep. Take.*) Suitcases? You've only come for tea!

ETHEL. (*The martyr.*) I've left him.

MILDRED. You've...left Humphrey? (*MILDRED looks shocked. She puts the suitcases down at the foot of the stairs. ETHEL nods.*) Oh, my goodness ... Ethel, I ... but he's rich! I mean ... oh, dear, dear, dear ... Sit down, love, let me take your coat ... What a shock ... (*Moves to hang up coat.*) I thought your marriage was such a happy one ...

ETHEL. About as happy as yours.

MILDRED. Oh, you poor thing!! (*Moves back to ETHEL.*) This is terrible! Terrible! I mean, I've got *four* portions of salmon ...

ETHEL. Then you'll have to put one back in the tin!

MILDRED. It's *fresh!* (*Controls herself.*) Would you like a glass of wine? That's fresh, too ...

ETHEL. Well, so long as it's vintage ...

MILDRED. Oh, it is ... I think. (*Reads from wine bottle label.*) "Mise En Bouteille aux Co-op Bottling Depot, Manchester."

ETHEL. Perhaps just a sip.

MILDRED. Yes, yes, of course. (*Brings over two glasses and the bottle of wine. During the following, she pours a glass for each of them.*) I mean, what happened? Was it something he said? You can tell me, I am your sister ...

ETHEL. I'd rather not talk about it.

MILDRED. (*Disappointed.*) No? Oh, well ... (*Sits on the settee.*) Yes ... there we are ... ahaha ... Mmm. How's the weather in Oxshott?

ETHEL. Fine, thank you. We had a little rain early this morning, but it cleared up very quickly and (*Breaks down. Sobs.*) He's having it off with his secretary!

MILDRED. There, there, there. Are you sure? (*Kneels by ETHEL.*)

ETHEL. (*Stiffly.*) Blonde hairs ... on his coat. He tried to blame them on our golden retriever.

MILDRED. Well, then ...

ETHEL. A golden retriever doesn't have black roots!

MILDRED. Ah.

ETHEL. The faith and trust has gone out of our marriage, Mildred. Whenever she phones, he rings off as soon as I pick up the extension.

MILDRED. Oh dear, dear.

ETHEL. And yesterday ... at four o'clock in the afternoon, he ... he called me by *her* name. "Jennifer," he said. "Jennifer."

MILDRED. Slip of the tongue, dear. (*Stands.*)

ETHEL. You don't know what he was doing at the time.

MILDRED. Well, no, but ... (*Surprise and envy.*) At four o'clock in the afternoon?

ETHEL. Oh, that's a regular thing. He always likes to get it over before The Wombles come on.

MILDRED. But they're on five times a week.

ETHEL. (*Long-suffering.*) You don't have to tell me. Stupid program! He's so demanding. You don't know what it's like, Mildred.

MILDRED. (*Wistful.*) No, I don't. No ...

ETHEL. You wouldn't think it to look at him.

MILDRED. No, you wouldn't. I will in future, though. (*A thought.*) They don't come on till twenty to six.

ETHEL. I know that.

MILDRED. Dear God ...

ETHEL. I'm sorry. I shouldn't burden you with my troubles.

MILDRED. Troubles ...? Yes ... look, love, I'll tell you what we're going to do. You'll stay here with us until you've sorted things out in your mind.

ETHEL. Oh, I shouldn't ask ...

MILDRED. Of course you should. After all, what are sisters for? Now, could you manage a little something to eat?

ETHEL. Perhaps just a morsel ... since it's fresh.

MILDRED. That's the way. Oh, you poor thing. (*Exits through the kitchen door, reenters immediately.*) What about Saturday and Sunday?

ETHEL. "New Faces" and "Songs of Praise."

MILDRED. Dear God ... (*Lays out plates. Brisk.*)

ETHEL. Shouldn't you ask George if it's all right for me to stay?

MILDRED. I don't think so, dear. I *know* what his answer will be. I'll wait for the right moment to tell him.

ETHEL. He'll see the suitcases.

MILDRED. Not him, love. He's not very observant.

GEORGE. (*Appears from the bedroom. He's changed his shirt, etc. The cuffs are flapping.*) Mildred ... Where are my cuff links?

MILDRED. (*Calling up.*) In your cuffs, George! (*To ETHEL.*) See what I mean? (*Exits to kitchen for GEORGE's fish.*)

GEORGE. (*Starts to come down the stairs, buttoning his cuffs, grumbling.*) Oh, yeah. I can't see the point in gettin' changed. That other shirt was perfectly clean, apart from a bit o'gravy. It's not as if we were ... (*He trips over the suitcases.*) Aaaagh! Gawd's strewth ... (*Picks himself up.*) Stupid place to leave suitcases! (*Crosses to dining table, vaguely nodding towards ETHEL.*) Hullo, Ethel, hullo, Humphrey.

(*MILDRED enters.*)

GEORGE. Where's me tea, then? (*Sits on US chair.*)
MILDRED. It's here, George. Would you like to take your place, Ethel? (*Places plate in front of GEORGE.*)
GEORGE. (*Looking at salmon.*) What's this?
MILDRED. Fish.
GEORGE. It's got no batter on it!
MILDRED. It's fresh salmon, George ... we have it often. (*Gay laugh.*) You sit here, Ethel ... by Prince Charles.
ETHEL. (*Sits on SL chair, baffled.*) Mmm? (*Realizes, looks at place mat dubiously.*) Oh, yes. Yes ... how loyal. I think he's in long trousers now.
MILDRED. We've had them for some time. (*She sits.*) The wine, George.
GEORGE. Eh? Oh, yeah ... (*Gets up, fetches the bottle of wine from the coffee table.*) I like a bit o'batter. Soaks up the vinegar and ... (*Pauses as a thought strikes him. Looks 'round, mentally*

counts the people present, making sure he's got his facts right.) Where's Humphrey?

MILDRED. Ah.

ETHEL. Er ...

MILDRED. He's not coming, George.

GEORGE. Oh, good. (*Heads back to the table with the wine.*) With chips and a pickled onion. Now that's a proper ... (*Pauses.*) Why not?

MILDRED. Well, er ...

ETHEL. Oh, he'll have to be told, Mildred. (*To GEORGE.*) 'Cos I've left him, that's why not.

GEORGE. What? You mean ... you and him...? You've (*Starts to cackle.*) Heehehe ... Heehehe ... oh, dear, dear, dear ... what a shame ... (*Sits, still cackling.*) Heehehe ... Still, these things happen. I'm sure you'll soon find somewhere nice. (*Long horrified pause.*) Suitcases?

MILDRED. Ethel's staying with us. Until she's made up her mind what she wants to do.

GEORGE. Now, hang on a minute, Mildred. I got nothin' against your sister ... she can't help the way she is ... but she's not staying here. No, no, no, no. Definitely not!

MILDRED. That's settled then, George! Now eat your fish. (*To ETHEL. Unctuous.*) *Do* have a little salad ...

(*GEORGE seethes, wagging a finger, but lost for words.*)

ETHEL. Thank you. Such a nice change from rich foods.

MILDRED. Yes ...

GEORGE. (*Standing.*) I am not having it, Mildred!

MILDRED. (*Indicating kitchen.*) Well, make yourself a sandwich!

GEORGE. I'm talking about *her!* We've only got the one bedroom!

ETHEL. If you think I'll be in the way ...

GEORGE. (*Grateful.*) Yes! Exactly! That's it! (*Sits.*) She understands.

MILDRED. She can share *our* bed, George!

GEORGE. It's not big enough ... !

MILDRED. You ... will be on the bed settee! (*Indicates it. GEORGE looks stricken. To ETHEL, all charm.*) Whoops ... I forgot the thin bread and butter! ... (*She exits to kitchen.*)

GEORGE. Mildred! I ... I ... oh. (*Sees she's gone. Frustrated, he drums his fingers. ETHEL continues to eat her salmon, rather smug.*) Oh ... (*To ETHEL.*) I ... I ... don't want to give the impression that ... that you're not welcome. (*ETHEL smiles stonily.*) No. It's just that ... I ... well, I ... (*An inspired thought.*) I had this idea! I'm takin' Mildred on a second honeymoon! Next Saturday!

ETHEL. What?

GEORGE. Yes, I've booked it! France! Bow-log-nee! I thought it'd give us a chance to recapture the magic an' romance an' all that rubbish ...

ETHEL. So I'll be left here on my own?

GEORGE. Yes. No! I ... y'see ... oh, gawd. Look, Ethel ... I'm tellin' you now, you will not enjoy sharing a bed with Mildred. I never have! You could puncture beer cans with her elbows ... And another thing, she *sighs* a lot. All night, sometimes ... she lies there ... sighin'.

ETHEL. I can understand that.

(*MILDRED comes in behind him, carrying a plate of bread and butter. She pauses, listening.*)

GEORGE. And grunting ... and moaning ... she makes all sorts o' funny noises ...

MILDRED. (*Clears throat, warningly.*) Ahum!

GEORGE. Yeah, that's the sort of ... (*Realizes.*) Ah ... er ... I was just ... I was just ...

MILDRED. Yes. (*She sits. To ETHEL.*) Here we are. Brown bread ... hand sliced.

ETHEL. Thank you. I must say the Co-op does quite a nice salmon.

MILDRED. The Co-op?

ETHEL. Mmm ... (*Fishes small stick-on label from her plate.*) "Ninety seven pee a quarter" (*With interest.*) "Frozen Food Department."

MILDRED. Ah, yes ...

GEORGE. I thought you said it was fresh?

MILDRED. It was! Before ... it was frozen. (*The DOORBELL rings. She looks grateful.*) Door, George!

GEORGE. Yeah, all right ... (*He stands and crosses to the front door.*) Hehehe ... you got caught out there, Mildred ... (*Looks out of the window.*) Here ... it's Humpty Dumpty! (*Starts to open front door.*)

ETHEL. I don't want to see him!

GEORGE. Oh, all right. We'll leave him out there ... (*Shuts front door and turns away.*)

MILDRED. George! (*To ETHEL.*) We can't just ...

ETHEL. I've got nothing to say to him. (*Stands, upset.*) We said it all this morning. He ... he called me a suspicious-minded old boot.

GEORGE. (*Admiring.*) He always did have a way with words. (*The DOORBELL rings again.*)

MILDRED. (*Consoling ETHEL.*) Never you mind, love. You come upstairs ... start unpacking ... perhaps have a little lie-down ... (*She leads the sniffling ETHEL up the stairs. They take one suitcase each.*)

ETHEL. (*To GEORGE.*) Tell him from me, he's a selfish pig.

GEORGE. Yes, right. Will do.

ETHEL. He can go down on his knees and grovel, but it won't make any difference.

GEORGE. Yes, I've got that.

ETHEL. I've given him the best years of my life and for what ... ?

GEORGE. Hang on ... I'd better write this down ...

MILDRED. Leave it, George! Can't you see she's upset? (*To ETHEL.*) There, there, there ... (*They exit to the bedroom, closing the door. The front DOORBELL rings again.*)

GEORGE. All right ... all right. (*He opens the front door to admit HUMPHREY. HUMPHREY is a middle-aged, self-made man. Well-dressed and sure of himself, he carries a big make-up case.*)

GEORGE. Come in, Humphrey.

HUMPHREY. Afternoon, George. I've brought this ... (*Hefts the case.*)

GEORGE. (*Dismay.*) You're not stayin' as well, are you?

HUMPHREY. It's for Ethel. It's her make-up.

GEORGE. Eh?

HUMPHREY. It's all in there. Plaster, lining paper, undercoat, topcoat ... matt, silk finish, gloss ... the lot. (*Sits on settee, dumps case beside it.*)

GEORGE. She won't be here that long. Oh, by the way, you're a selfish pig.

HUMPHREY. What?

GEORGE. And you can go down on your knees and grovel ... it won't make any difference. (*He collects his plate of salmon and crosses to sit by HUMPHREY, eating it.*)

HUMPHREY. I see. Anything else?

GEORGE. There was a bit more, but it was all along the same lines (*Interested.*) Listen, what did you *do* to get your wife to pack up an' leave you?

HUMPHREY. (*Reluctant.*) Oh ...

GEORGE. No, c'mon, tell me. It could come in very handy, that.

HUMPHREY. I didn't do anything, George! She's jealous, that's all. Imagines things. Thinks I'm having affairs right, left and center.

GEORGE. You must have done *something*.

HUMPHREY. No, nothing! I admit I'm as highly sexed as the next man, but ...

GEORGE. I'm the next man.

HUMPHREY. Yes, well ... as you were. But it's all in her mind, George ...

GEORGE. Yeah ... (*A thought.*) Here, she can't be *that* jealous if she's left you on your own with the au pair girl.

HUMPHREY. Consuela? She's built like a Dalek, George! And she's got a better moustache than you have! (*GEORGE fingers his moustache unhappily. MILDRED enters from the bedroom, closing the door. She comes down the stairs.*)

HUMPHREY. Tell you the truth, I don't think Ethel'd mind if I *was* spreading it about a bit. Take some of the load off her. She's not a ... (*Sees MILDRED.*) Oh ... afternoon, Mildred.

MILDRED. (*Eyeing him speculatively, intrigued.*) Hullo, Humphrey. Ahaha ... Well,

well, well ... and how are you ... Mmmm? (*She sits beside him on the settee, her manner slightly coquettish.*)

HUMPHREY. Oh, pretty fit, y'know. I look after myself.

MILDRED. (*Knowing.*) Yes. Ahahaha ... Yes. Get Humphrey a drink, George.

GEORGE. (*Stands.*) Um ... glass o' water, Humphrey?

HUMPHREY. Whisky and soda, please.

GEORGE. Whisky? Cor blimey ... (*Crosses to sideboard, puts down plate. Opens cupboard, takes out half-full bottle of scotch, resentful.*) It's fifty bob a bottle this, y'know. (*Blows dust off the bottle.*)

HUMPHREY. Fifty bob?

MILDRED. It was when he bought that one.

GEORGE. Right ... damned expensive stuff!

MILDRED. Swearbox!

GEORGE. Oh ... (*Puts coin in the swearbox, grumbling.*) I'm fed up with this blasted thing!

MILDRED. And again.

GEORGE. Oh ... (*Another coin.*)

MILDRED. (*To HUMPHREY, amused.*) Last year I got a real leather handbag out of that pig. (*GEORGE reacts.*)

HUMPHREY. Very nice.

MILDRED. When he saw the bill, he nearly filled it again. (*Chuckles.*)

(*HUMPHREY also chuckles. GEORGE pours him a minute scotch and a large squirt of soda. During the following, he brings it over and hands it to HUMPHREY.*)

HUMPHREY. I'll say one thing for you, Mildred ... you've got a sense of humor. (*He puts his hand on her knee, patting it.*)

MILDRED. (*Thrilled.*) Oh ... (*The Grandmother clock on the landing STRIKES four. MILDRED and HUMPHREY both turn to look up at it as it strikes.*)

GEORGE. (*Checking his own watch, dour.*) Um ... four o'clock.

MILDRED. Yes ... (*Laughs gaily.*) Four o'clock ... ahaha ...

HUMPHREY. (*Shifting restlessly.*) Aye ... Four o'clock ... I'm usually getting in about now.

MILDRED. So I believe. (*Looks at his hand on her knee. Recalls herself.*) Ice, George! For Humphrey! For Humphrey's drink!

GEORGE. Tch! I dunno ... Hand me ... fetch me ... carry me ... (*He exits to the kitchen, grumbling.*)

HUMPHREY. (*Clears throat. Removes hand from her knee. Indicates.*) Is she ... er ... is she upstairs?

MILDRED. Yes, she's having a little lie-down.

HUMPHREY. Ah. She usually does, about this time.

MILDRED. So I understand. (*Pulls herself together. Looks firm.*) Humphrey, Ethel *is* my sister and I *am* very fond of her. So I feel entitled to ask ... is there any truth in what she says? About you and ... your secretary?

HUMPHREY. (*Flatly.*) Miss Frazer ...

MILDRED. Jennifer.

HUMPHREY. (*Impatient.*) Yes ... I think that's her name. Tch ... is she still going on about that? It's fantasy. Dear me ... (*Shakes head sadly.*) No, that's not what this is all about. She's leaving me because ... well, there are certain things I like that she ... isn't so keen on.

MILDRED. Wombling.

HUMPHREY. What? Well, I've never heard it called that before but ... All I'm saying is that ... I'm a red-blooded man, Mildred, and I like a ... I enjoy a ... do I have to spell it out?

MILDRED. No, I know how it's spelt.

HUMPHREY. And Ethel doesn't enjoy it, and that's what the real problem is!

MILDRED. I see.

GEORGE. (*Enters from the kitchen. He's got a handkerchief wrapped around his finger and a vulgar, tasteless ice bucket.*) Strewth! It's murder gettin' them ice cubes out the tray! (*Dumps the ice bucket on the coffee table.*)

MILDRED. You should have used a knife.

GEORGE. I did.

HUMPHREY. (*Helps himself. Plops a couple of ice cubes into his scotch.*) Thanks, George.

GEORGE. I cut me finger. That's why there's blood all over the ice.

HUMPHREY. Eh? (*Looks in ice bucket, then at his drink. Disgusted, he lays it aside and sighs.*) Urgh ...

GEORGE. (*Sits on armchair, putting his feet up on the coffee table.*) Now then, you *are* takin' Ethel home with you, aren't you?

HUMPHREY. It's up to her, George.

GEORGE. No. Oh, no. You are the husband ... the master. The husband tells the wife what to do ... not the other way round.

MILDRED. Feet off the table.

(*He takes them off automatically, not really conscious of the interruption. He crosses his legs.*)

GEORGE. (*To HUMPHREY.*) Man is the dominant partner ...

MILDRED. Don't cross your legs, you'll crease your trousers.

GEORGE. (*Uncrosses his legs.*) ... out, hunting the dinosaur, while the little woman ...

MILDRED. And sit up straight! (*To HUMPHREY.*) I'll get you another scotch.

GEORGE. D'you mind, Mildred? I'm speakin'!

MILDRED. (*Standing.*) Oh, shut up. (*She crosses to the sideboard and pours another scotch and soda during the following.*)

GEORGE. (*Faltering.*) While ... the little woman ... er ... Well, I think I've made my point. (*Clears throat.*)

(*ETHEL comes out of the bedroom. The martyr.*)

HUMPHREY. I know you mean well, George, but Ethel is not ... (*Sees her. Stands.*) Oh, hullo, love.
ETHEL. (*Coming downstairs. Frosty.*) You're still here, are you?
HUMPHREY. Er ... yes.
ETHEL. You're wasting your time! I'm not coming home with you. I've had enough. I've had more than enough! You ... you womanizer! (*Takes the glass of whisky from MILDRED and has a swig. MILDRED looks surprised.*) Thank you. (*Back to HUMPHREY.*) You can go. Go back to your detached house with its heated swimming pool and its three-car garage. I'd rather stay in a hovel ... (*Gestures about her.*)
MILDRED. (*To self.*) Oh, thank you. (*To ETHEL.*) Well, I'm sure you two have got plenty to chat about. We'll leave you to it. Come on, George. (*Picks up some dishes from the table.*)
GEORGE. I wanna stay an' listen.
MILDRED. Out! (*Indicates kitchen.*)
GEORGE. (*Grumbles as he goes.*) Nyaa ...
MILDRED. You're mumbling again!

(*They exit to the kitchen. ETHEL sits, tight-lipped. HUMPHREY paces about, trying to reason with her.*)

HUMPHREY. Ethel ... oh, look, is it because I haven't been paying you enough attention ... is that it?
ETHEL. No! That is *not* it!
HUMPHREY. Oh. Have I been paying you too *much?*
ETHEL. I have always accepted that that side of marriage is important to you.
HUMPHREY. Yes. But you're not ... enthusiastic.
ETHEL. Not while I'm in the middle of pruning the roses, no. Those secateurs finished up three gardens away.
HUMPHREY. Well, if it's not that, what is it?
ETHEL. You know perfectly well.
HUMPHREY. You're not still on about Miss Frazer?
ETHEL. Oh, it's "Miss Frazer" now, is it? At four o'clock yesterday it was "Jennifer, Jennifer!"
HUMPHREY. (*Sits, impatient.*) I didn't say "Jennifer," I said "Pinafore."
ETHEL. (*Skeptical.*) And why would you cry "Pinafore" at an ... intimate moment like that?
HUMPHREY. Because it was getting in my way!

ETHEL. Hah! We'll see if my solicitor believes you.

HUMPHREY. Solicitor?

ETHEL. Oh, yes. I'm taking the matter further.

HUMPHREY. (*Stands, losing patience.*) Oh, do what you like! But I'll tell you this ... you're making a mistake. I have never looked at another woman in my life! (*Heads for front door.*)

ETHEL. I don't believe you.

HUMPHREY. Have it your own way! Consuela ... here I come! Ole´! (*He exits. She looks after him, stunned.*)

ETHEL. (*Calls.*) You know your trouble? You're a ... a ... (*Gropes for words.*)

GEORGE. (*Sticks his head and shoulder through the kitchen hatch.*) Like a cuppa tea?

ETHEL. (*Turning on GEORGE.*) ... sex maniac!

(*The hatch slips down, trapping GEORGE. He squeals.*)

CURTAIN

ACT I

Scene 2

SCENE: The morning of the following Saturday, about nine a.m. The dining table is now folded and stacked underneath the hatch, with the dining chairs on either side of it. The settee has been opened out into a double bed.

AT RISE: GEORGE is asleep and snoring under a tangled heap of bedclothes. He has obviously had a restless night. His clothes are heaped on the armchair. He mumbles and stirs, then settles down again. The letterbox rattles and a morning newspaper. ("The Sun") plops onto the front doormat.

He grunts and sits up, waking. He throws aside the bedclothes and sits on the side of the bed, yawning and scrabbling for a cigarette. He lights one and enjoys a cough and a scratch. He stands and hobbles over to the front door, slightly bent and grunting in pain from his back. He's wearing crumpled pyjamas and socks.

He picks up the newspaper.

GEORGE. Page three ... (*Opens newspaper and reads aloud as he heads back to the bed,*

WHEN THE CAT'S AWAY 35

dropping the letters on the coffee table.) Ah ... "Wendy 42-34-36. Um ... She is studying to be a model and obviously has great things in front of her ..." Yes. (*Thinks about it, then chuckles.*) Hehehehe ... witty, that. (*Climbs back into bed.*) I dunno how they think them up ...

MILDRED. (*Enters from the bedroom. She's wearing a smart going-away outfit. She comes downstairs carrying a suitcase.*) George ...

GEORGE. (*Hastily turning page.*) I see the pound is buoyant on the international money market.

MILDRED. Will you get up! I'm not taking you to France in your pyjamas!

GEORGE. You're not taking me to France at all!

MILDRED. ... Get up! How do you think Ethel feels, seeing you half naked every morning?

GEORGE. (*Slyly.*) Y' reckon I'm gettin' her over-excited, do you?

MILDRED. Don't be pathetic! (*Puts her suitcase on the armchair.*)

GEORGE. Ah, now, come on, Mildred ... (*Strokes his moustache.*) It has been remarked that I have certain things in common with Ronald Colman.

MILDRED. You have! He's been dead for years! Now, get out of that bed, or I'll climb in with you!

GEORGE. (*Springs out of the bed with alacrity.*) I'm out! I'm out! But I'm still not coming with you! (*During the following he puts on a tatty dressing gown and his slippers. She briskly tidies the bedclothes.*)

MILDRED. We'll see. How on earth you get these sheets in such a ... (*She finds a jar and a packet under the pillow.*) "Pickled onions?" "Cream Crackers?" Oh, you're enjoying your little self down here, aren't you?

GEORGE. It has its compensations. I can move me legs about without it being misunderstood.

MILDRED. Give me a hand. (*He helps her straighten the bedclothes.*) I want this place tidy before Ethel comes down.

GEORGE. Oh, Ethel ... (*Mumbles darkly.*)

MILDRED. What did you say?

GEORGE. I'm not telling you. You'll make me put money in that thing. (*Indicates swearbox.*)

MILDRED. You really resent her being here, don't you? You've been making it obvious all week. I've seen you ... dropping your chewing gum in her tea.

GEORGE. Well ... she's in the way, Mildred. (*Indicates W.C.*) If I wanna go to the loo, she's in there. (*Indicates bathroom.*) If I wanna go to the bathroom, she's in there. And she forgot to lock the door yesterday!

MILDRED. I know. I heard the scream.

WHEN THE CAT'S AWAY

GEORGE. I couldn't help it. Frightened the life out o'me.

MILDRED. You didn't have to strike up a conversation with her.

GEORGE. It was an embarrassing moment. I was trying to smooth things over.

MILDRED. By discussing her appendix scar?

GEORGE. She didn't have a lot else that was worth talking about.

MILDRED. (*Thrusts pillows at him.*) Sideboard.

GEORGE. Yes. (*Wheedling.*) When she's going back to him, Mildred?

MILDRED. When she thinks he's suffered enough.

GEORGE. But he isn't sufferin' at all. She's stayin' here! I'm the one who's suffering. (*He puts the pillows in the sideboard. Returns. They fold the bed back into a settee.*) It's only because of her that you make me dress for dinner.

MILDRED. I'd hardly call putting a shirt on "dressing for dinner!"

GEORGE. I don't like her.

MILDRED. George, she is my sister. We grew up together ... (*Sits on the arm of the armchair, becoming sentimental.*) We shared our childhood. I used to wear her dresses after she'd grown out of them ... She let me have her toys when she'd finished with them ... We even had a crush on the same boy at school. He used to carry my books until ... he met Ethel. (*Hardens.*) I don't like her, either, but she's my sister! (*She stands and exits to the kitchen.*)

GEORGE. (*Calls after her.*) I think Humpty's right. He knows her better than either of us ... and I agree with him. She's an old ... (*Turns to see ETHEL coming from the bathroom.*) ... boot-tiful morning, Ethel.

ETHEL. (*Wearing a frilly, feminine, rather expensive dress. She sweeps regally downstairs.*) I suppose so.

GEORGE. You sleepin' all right, are you?

ETHEL. Not really. Mildred's very restless. Keeps flinging her arm across me.

GEORGE. Oh, yeah. She does that with me.

ETHEL. I wondered whether to wake her up.

GEORGE. Oh, no. That's the worst thing you can do! She gets frisky, know what I mean?

ETHEL. Yes, indeed. Humphrey's the same.

GEORGE. Here, speakin' of Humphrey. When are you going to go back to him?

ETHEL. When he gets down on his knees and begs my forgiveness!

GEORGE. Ah ... (*Sits to read newspaper.*) I thought you said that wouldn't make any difference?

ETHEL. That was before I'd had a week of Mildred's elbows and you ogling me in the bath!

MILDRED. (*Comes from the kitchen.*) Oh, you're down. The kettle's on. (*Eyes her outfit, jealously.*) Is that a new dress?

ETHEL. (*Smug.*) Yes. It's one of Pierre Cardin's ...

GEORGE. Same size as you, is he? Hehehe ... Just my little joke ... hehehe ...

ETHEL. Yes, I've heard about your little joke.

(*Uncertain what she means, GEORGE looks suspiciously at MILDRED.*)

MILDRED. (*Hastily.*) Ah! The tickets! For our flight! Ahaha ... If we leave fairly soon ...

GEORGE. (*Disbelief.*) Mildred ... tch, it's like talking to a brick wall ... I've told you! I'm not goin'!

MILDRED. George, I've booked! I've got the foreign currency ... I've got the tickets. If you didn't want to go, you should have said so.

GEORGE. (*Splutters.*) I *did!* I heard myself!

MILDRED. That's settled then, good. (*To ETHEL.*) The flight's at one o'clock, so we really should leave as soon as ...

GEORGE. Hang on! I said I'm not going!

MILDRED. That's right, George. You're not going. (*To ETHEL.*) ... as soon as we've had a quick cuppa ...

ETHEL. (*Enthusiastic.*) We must try and visit one of the vineyards.

MILDRED. Yes ... and there's one or two little restaurants you'll *love!*

ETHEL. Oh, I adore French food ...

MILDRED. So do I ...

GEORGE. (*Has been looking from one to the other, baffled.*) Just a minute! What ... what ... what's it got to do with her?

MILDRED. She's coming with me, George. No point in wasting the ticket.

ETHEL. I shall pay my own way. (*To MILDRED.*) There's a little boutique in Lyon ...

MILDRED. I know! You mentioned it!

ETHEL. The most gorgeous silk scarves ... and the shoes ...!

MILDRED. (*Thrilled.*) Ooh ... !

GEORGE. Tup ... tup ... tuptch ... What about *me?*

MILDRED. You can stay here, George. Have the house to yourself. You've been complaining all week it's over-crowded.

GEORGE. Strewth! (*Stands.*) That's marvelous, innit? She's pinched me bed ... now she's pinching me second honeymoon.

MILDRED. You said you didn't want to go!

GEORGE. No, I didn't! Not in so many words ... (*Accusingly.*) You two have got it all worked out!

ETHEL. I've no wish to come between husband and wife ...

MILDRED. Don't worry, love. There's yards of room! (*To GEORGE.*) All right. Here is your last chance! Are you coming with me or are you not?

GEORGE. (*Cunning.*) Aha! So that's what this is all about. (*Dry chuckle.*) I see through your

WHEN THE CAT'S AWAY 41

little game ... it's all a bluff, innit? Just to get me to say I'll go. Well, I won't! Hehehe ... so what you gonna do now?

MILDRED. I'll go with Ethel. (*A kettle WHISTLES in the kitchen. She stands. To ETHEL.*) Tea and toast?

ETHEL. Yes, please. My Earl Grey. And my Fortnum and Mason wholemeal.

MILDRED. Of course. (*Exits to kitchen.*)

GEORGE. (*Calling after her, losing confidence.*) No, no ... y'see ... I called your bluff there, Mildred. I mean ... I ... (*To ETHEL.*) I called her bluff, see ... erm ... Oh. (*He sits beside her.*) It's ridiculous. Second honeymoon at our age. You wouldn't ask Humphrey for a second honeymoon, would you?

ETHEL. (*With feeling.*) God forbid!

GEORGE. There you are, then.

ETHEL. (*Softening.*) Look George ... I know you and I haven't always got on very well, but ... I am a guest in your house and I feel I've imposed enough ...

GEORGE. True.

ETHEL. Well, I meant what I said. I didn't want to come between a husband and wife ... (*Instantly fearful.*) God knows, I know what it's like when another woman comes between a husband ... and ... and ... oh (*Stifled sob.*)

GEORGE. Now, now, don't start the waterworks ... (*Calls off.*) Mildred! (*To ETHEL.*) Look, I'm not bothered ... I mean ... I got a hanky here somewhere ... (*He fumbles in his dressing gown pocket, half pulls out a piece of material.*)

ETHEL. (*Sobs.*) Mildred just thought ... a little holiday might help me see things in perspective ... Thank you.

(*She reaches across, gropes for and takes the piece of material from his hand. Turns away. She goes to dab her eyes with it. We and GEORGE realize that it's the hem of his pyjama jacket, that he's inadvertently pulled through a hole in his dressing gown pocket.*)

ETHEL. And since you didn't seem to want to go ...

GEORGE. Er ... no, not really. Thing is, y'see ... er ... erm. (*Tries to draw her attention to the fact that she's dabbling her eyes with his pyjamas.*) I ... er ... that's my ... er ... Look, you go, Ethel! I don't mind ... but, the thing is, you got hold o' my wotsit ...

ETHEL. I'll be all right in a minute. (*She blows her nose on the corner of his pyjama jacket.*) Thank you. (*She hands the piece of material back to GEORGE. He looks at it gloomily.*)

GEORGE. Thank *you!* Cor blimey ... (*Stands, with his back to the kitchen, opens his dressing gown wide to show her what she's done.*) Look at that? Innit marvelous ... !

WHEN THE CAT'S AWAY

(During the above, MILDRED enters from the kitchen, carrying a small tray containing tea and toast.)

MILDRED. George ...! What are you *doing?*
GEORGE. Eh?
ETHEL. He was just being kind, Mildred ... *(Picks up the newspaper.)*
GEORGE. It's the last time I offer *her* anything! *(Heads for the W.C.)* That's probably stained my pyjamas, that has. *(Returns and snatches the paper from ETHEL, then exits to the W.C. with it.)*
MILDRED. *(Baffled.)* Yes, well ... tea and toast. *(Puts it on the coffee table.)*
ETHEL. Thank you. *(Nibbles at the toast, sips the tea.)* The last time I was in France, I had an improper suggestion made to me on the beach.
MILDRED. *(Fascinated.)* Really? How dreadful? What did he say? *(She's crossed to the front door, and now brings in a bottle of milk from the doorstep.)*
ETHEL. I don't know. It was all in French.
MILDRED. Oh. Then how did you know it was ...
ETHEL. He did drawings in the sand with his loaf.
MILDRED. *(Thrilled.)* Disgraceful. Which beach was this? *(Sits beside ETHEL, adds milk to her own tea.)*

ETHEL. Oh, they're all the same. You have to watch out for that sort of thing.

MILDRED. I certainly will, yes. (*Looks at her watch.*) Actually, we don't want to miss the plane.

ETHEL. Um? Good heavens, yes. I better finish packing. (*Heads upstairs to the bedroom, taking her coffee with her.*) That's all the French ever think about. That's why there's so many of them.

MILDRED. Yes. I see what you mean. (*ETHEL exits to the bedroom, closing the door.*) Oohoo ... (*She crosses to her suitcase, opens it. She glances 'round, then takes a bikini top from the case. She tries it against herself, wriggles with excitement at her own daring.*) Oohoo ... (*Dreamily.*) Ooh ... Bonjour, Jean-Paul. Je suis ... er ... je suis ... fancy-free! (*Turns the other way.*) Pardon, Pierre? Moi? Et tu? Back to your place? Ah, no, no, no, no. Naughty boy!

(*During the above, HUMPHREY has appeared at the partly open front door. He carries a bunch of flowers. He looks at MILDRED, amazed, then clears his throat.*)

HUMPHREY. Harrumph ...
MILDRED. (*Flustered.*) Ah, Humphrey ... bonjour ... er ... hullo.
HUMPHREY. Hullo, Mildred. I was just passing ... thought I'd drop by ... see if Ethel's come to her senses yet.

MILDRED. Ah, yes ... do sit down. (*Hastily removes bikini top and stuffs it in the case.*) Aha ... I'll move the suitcase. (*She moves the case onto the armchair.*)

HUMPHREY. You going somewhere?

MILDRED. Flying to France. Second honeymoon.

HUMPHREY. Ah ... I thought George didn't like flying. (*Sits.*)

MILDRED. He's not coming.

HUMPHREY. Oh. (*Holds up flowers.*) I've brought these ... she ... (*Take.*) Isn't it a bit pointless? If he's not with you?

MILDRED. Ethel's coming. (*HUMPHREY reacts.*) It's more of a *holiday*, really.

HUMPHREY. I should hope so. (*Realizes.*) Ethel? To France?

(*During the above, ETHEL has come from the bedroom, wearing a fur coat and carrying a suitcase. She sees HUMPHREY and comes down.*)

ETHEL. (*Frostily.*) So, *you're* here, are you? You've condescended to drop in ... see if I'm still alive.

HUMPHREY. (*Stands.*) Yes, love. Are you? Uh ... *how* are you? (*Gives her flowers.*)

ETHEL. I'm fine, thank you ... Rested.

HUMPHREY. Good, good. Well, I came to take you home ...

ETHEL. Oh, did you? And what about you and Consuela?

HUMPHREY. (*Exasperated.*) Oh, for ... that was a joke! (*To MILDRED.*) You've seen her.. (*To ETHEL.*) ... daughter of Godzilla!

MILDRED. Ethel, dear ... if you'd rather go home with Humphrey ...

HUMPHREY. Right, that's settled, then. Come home, we'll go out tonight! I've booked a table at your favorite Italian restaurant ...

ETHEL. (*Cool.*) Oh, have you?

HUMPHREY. ... that little trattoria ... in Fulham ... where the guitarist gave you the rose, remember? And I tucked it in your hair and ... and ... (*Loses confidence as he sees her stony expression.*) ...and you ... er ... you ...

ETHEL. I have never been to an Italian restaurant in Fulham in my life! (*Drops the flowers on the coffee table.*)

MILDRED. Whoops! Faux pas! Sorry ... just practicing my French. (*Heads for bedroom.*) I'll get the other suitcase ... (*Exits to bedroom.*)

HUMPHREY. No. No ... I, er ... believe you're right, Ethel. It wasn't you. It was a ... it was a client. Mr. ... ah ... Mr. Thomson, Sid Thomson.

ETHEL. And you tucked a rose in his hair.

HUMPHREY. I ... may have exaggerated that bit ...

ETHEL. (*Stiffly.*) It was *her*, wasn't it? It was Jennifer.

WHEN THE CAT'S AWAY 47

HUMPHREY. No, no. No! Sid Thomson's nothing like her! He's bald. Well ... he's got enough hair to tuck a rose in, but ...

ETHEL. Oh, what a tangled web we weave.

HUMPHREY. Look, we won't go there. We'll go to that Japanese one, where they serve the wind-dried ... (*Sudden doubt.*) We have been to a Japanese restaurant, haven't we?

ETHEL. Yes.

HUMPHREY. Oh, good. We'll go again! And then ...

ETHEL. Humphrey, I am going to France with my sister. While I am away, I will consider my position ...

(*GEORGE comes from the downstairs W.C. F/X toilet flushing, but not loudly. He carries a folded newspaper and a pencil. He's dressed in trousers, cardigan, etc.*)

GEORGE. Ah ... four-letter word ... oh, hullo, Humphrey. Can you think of a four-letter word ...

(*MILDRED comes from the bedroom, carrying another suitcase. She comes downstairs.*)

HUMPHREY. No problem at all, George.

GEORGE. (*Reading clue.*) "Footwear named after Wellington?"

HUMPHREY. Boot!

GEORGE. Oh, yeah! (*Looks at ETHEL, fills it in.*) Yeah!

MILDRED. (*Looking through window.*) The taxi's here! (*To ETHEL.*) I do think we ought to be going ... if we *are* going, that is.

ETHEL. Well, I'm ready. (*Picks up suitcase.*)

HUMPHREY. (*Pleading.*) Ethel ... (*Takes suitcase from her.*) Why don't we just ... Ethel! (*ETHEL marches out of the front door. HUMPHREY goes to follow.*)

MILDRED. If you wouldn't mind, Humphrey? (*Indicates her suitcases.*)

HUMPHREY. What? Oh ... yes. (*Picks them up, then follows ETHEL out.*) Ethel! Can't we talk about it ... ?

MILDRED. (*Turns to GEORGE, who's still considering his crossword.*) Well, George, I'm going.

GEORGE. (*Not looking up.*) Enjoy yourself.

MILDRED. Make sure you eat properly ... don't watch too much television ... oh, and don't forget to change your underwear.

GEORGE. (*Looking up.*) I won't need to. You're only goin' for a week.

MILDRED. (*Sighs. Gives him piece of paper.*) That's the address and phone number of the hotel. Will you miss me?

GEORGE. Oh, yeah. Yeah. S'funny, really ... you on your second honeymoon ... and I'll be miles away.

MILDRED. You were miles away on our first, George. Now, come on, bite the bullet, kiss me goodbye.

GEORGE. (*Reluctantly.*) Umm ... right. (*Gives her a peck on the cheek.*) There!

MILDRED. Oh, thank you. Done with all the passion of a sparrow attacking a crust.

HUMPHREY. (*Mooches in.*) Ethel wants to know if you're coming ... says there's no time to hang about.

MILDRED. I've been telling *her* that ... oh ... 'Bye, Humphrey. 'Bye George, I'll send you a postcard. (*She exits. HUMPHREY and GEORGE look out after her.*)

GEORGE. 'Bye ... (*An afterthought.*) Oh, when you take out the flight insurance, put it in my name ... 'Bye!

HUMPHREY. 'Bye. (*GEORGE shuts the front door.*) Ah, well ... (*Reaches for his hip pocket.*) Fancy a good stiff scotch, George?

GEORGE. I wouldn't mind. Ta.

HUMPHREY. (*Indicating sideboard.*) The bottle's in the sideboard. (*Takes out cigarette case.*)

GEORGE. Oh, yeah ... um. S'pose so. Bit *early*, innit? (*HUMPHREY sits on the arm of the chair. GEORGE pours a couple of scotch and sodas.*)

HUMPHREY. Only in England.

GEORGE. Um ... well, I s'pose so ... Did you come 'round for any reason at all?

HUMPHREY. (*Sighs.*) Aye. I came to get Ethel back.

GEORGE. What for?

HUMPHREY. I don't know, Geo ... well, I *do* know. I saw my solicitors yesterday afternoon.

GEORGE. Ah ... (*Bringing drinks.*) Here y'are. You don't want ice in it, do you?

HUMPHREY. (*Hastily covering glass.*) No! No ... thanks. George. D'you know what they said? If me and Ethel split up ... she can take damn near every penny I've got!

GEORGE. Tch, tch, tch. Swearbox! (*Picks up swearbox.*)

HUMPHREY. Eh? It doesn't apply to me.

GEORGE. No. Ah ... (*A thought.*) Here, it doesn't apply to me either. Not now. (*He snickers gleefully, shakes the box up and down.*) I can say anything I like! Hehehe ... I could say ... er ... ooh! I could say ... I could say ... (*Dismay.*) There's no fun in it when it's free.

HUMPHREY. (*Long-suffering.*) I was talking, George.

GEORGE. Oh, sorry. (*Puts box down on coffee table.*) Every penny you got ... go on.

HUMPHREY. It's all in her name, y'see. For tax purposes. The house, the car, three o' the shops ... all in her name. If she divorces me, well ... I've *got* to have her back! (*Brightens.*) But not for a week, thank God. (*Swigs his scotch.*)

GEORGE. You don't miss her, then?

HUMPHREY. Oh, I admit there are times when I feel like ... wombling free, so to speak. (*Stands. Makes decision.*) Can I use your phone, George?

GEORGE. (*Surly.*) Oh, yes. Anything y'like.

HUMPHREY. Good lad. I'll have another scotch. (*Gives GEORGE his glass and heads for the phone.*)

GEORGE. (*Grumbles his way back to the sideboard, pours drink.*)

HUMPHREY. (*Dialling.*) The way I look at it, once Ethel gets back, I'll really have to watch my p's and q's ... She gets these wild, unjustified suspicions about me and other women. I don't ... (*To phone, intimate.*) Hullo, Jennifer. It's Lover Boy!

(*GEORGE looks up from pouring his drinks, surprised. During the following he wanders over to the phone with HUMPHREY's drink.*)

HUMPHREY. (*To phone.*) Yes ... Listen, I'm free tonight ... and I've booked a table at our favorite Italian restaurant ... the little trattoria in Fulham, remember? Where the guitarist gave you the rose and I tucked it in your hair? Yes! It was you! Good! Well ...

GEORGE. Oo's that, then? Madame Cholet or Orinoco?

HUMPHREY. Eh?

GEORGE. Nothing. I'm going for a shave. Shut the front door when you go. (*Exits to bathroom.*)

HUMPHREY. Yes, yes. (*To phone.*) Tell you what, I'll pick you up tonight, about ... erh? Shirley ... oh. Can't you tell her you're going out? (*Listens.*) I see, yes ... Oh, I'm sure she doesn't mean it. People who say they're going to commit ... well, they're never the ones who *do* ... No ... no ... Can't you just put her on the phone to the Samaritans and sneak out while she's ... No? Oh. Um? I can't take *both* of you, Jennifer. I ... (*A thought.*) Unless we make up a foursome. Mm? Well, as it happens, I *do* know someone, yes ... (*Glances towards kitchen.*) Oh, he's late thirty ... ish. He's got more than a touch of Ronald Colman. Film star ... (*Irritable.*) He was with Zasu Pitts in ... Zasu Pitts! Oh, let it go! I'll pick you up at ... yes, *both* of you..at six thirty. All right? 'Bye. 'Bye ... (*Kiss to phone. Phone down.*)

(*HUMPHREY paces thoughtfully. GEORGE comes in from the bathroom. He's taken off his dressing gown, but is still in pyjamas. He's got a razor and a large tube of shaving cream. He's dabbing the shaving cream on his chin.*)

GEORGE. Oh, by the way, Humphrey ... just leave the two pence beside the phone.

HUMPHREY. Oh, yes, right. (*Leaves a coin.*) Er ... can I have a word with you, George? (*Beckons him.*)

GEORGE. (*Coming downstairs.*) What about?

HUMPHREY. Well, I've been thinking. (*Puts arm around him.*) We don't see enough of each other, you and I.

GEORGE. Yes we do.

HUMPHREY. No. I mean we're brothers-in-law ... and how long is it since I last took you out for a slap-up meal at my expense, eh?

GEORGE. Never.

HUMPHREY. Exactly! And it's beginning to prey on my mind.

GEORGE. (*Puzzling it through.*) Hang on. I thought you and your ... er ... your wossname ... (*Indicates phone.*) I thought you were takin' her out ... ?

HUMPHREY. I am, George. And we'd like you to join us.

GEORGE. Er ... wouldn't I be playin' raspberry?

HUMPHREY. You, George? With your magnetic personality and bubbling wit? No. I don't mind telling you, you'd make the evening for me.

GEORGE. (*Believes every word.*) Oh, yeah, well, hehehe ... yeah. Magnetic personality ... yeah. You're one o' the few people who have spotted that.

HUMPHREY. Incredible. That's settled, then. The four of us will have a great evening. I'll pick you up about six ... better put a tie on ...

GEORGE. (*Going upstairs.*) Right. I got one for my birthday that goes very well with my ... (*Swivels and comes back down the stairs in one smooth movement.*) Four?

HUMPHREY. Didn't I mention? She's bringing her flat-mate, Shirley ... nice girl.

GEORGE. I'm not going! (*Sits on settee, folds arms.*)

HUMPHREY. George ... let's not be hasty.

GEORGE. No. I know what this sort o' thing can lead to, Humphrey. Starts out as a friendly little meal ... glass o' wine ... ends up, they expect something for it.

HUMPHREY. (*Baffled.*) Eh?

GEORGE. They get you into a shop doorway, or an air raid shelter ...

HUMPHREY. They what?

GEORGE. ... want you to *do* things.

HUMPHREY. If it'll set your mind at rest, there aren't many air raid shelters left in Fulham ...

GEORGE. No, I'm not going.

HUMPHREY. How about if I ask you nicely?

GEORGE. No.

HUMPHREY. How about if I threaten you?

GEORGE. No ... Eh?

HUMPHREY. (*Prodding GEORGE with finger.*) In a week's time, Ethel will be back.

Now, I can take her home straight away ... or I can leave her here. With you. For another month.

(*A long pause as GEORGE considers this. Goes to make several points, but decides against it every time. Eventually ...*)

GEORGE. You think I ought to put a tie on, then. (*He stands.*)
HUMPHREY. Good man! Oh, and just in case you luck's in ... better put on a clean pair of underpants! (*Slaps him on the back, chuckling.*)
GEORGE. (*Fearful whinny.*) Nyaaa ... ! (*He inadvertently squeezes the large tube. A gout of shaving cream shoots high in the air.*)

CURTAIN

ACT II

Scene 2

Later same evening, about midnight. The room is in darkness, apart from street LIGHTING through the window. Sounds of MERRIMENT outside.

HUMPHREY/JENNIFER. (*Off.*) Aye, aye, conga ... aye, aye, conga ... (*Etc.*)

(*SCRAPE of the key in the front door and HUMPHREY and JENNIFER conga in, turning on the LIGHT. They've both had a few drinks and are a little merry. HUMPHREY carries two bottles of champagne. He has a flower behind his ear. They leave the door open. JENNIFER is in her mid-twenties, an attractive blonde, dressed for an evening out, relaxed and enjoying herself. They conga round the room and HUMPHREY puts the bottles down on the coffee table. JENNIFER has a handbag with a strap.*)

HUMPHREY/ JENNIFER. Aye, aye, conga ... ooh! Aye, aye, conga ... Ooh ... (*Etc.*

HUMPHREY swivels JENNIFER round and they give each other a big kiss.)
HUMPHREY. Weh-hey-hey ... Mmmm.

(*After a moment, GEORGE enters through the front door, with SHIRLEY behind him. They are also attempting the conga, but with markedly less enthusiasm. Small steps and their heart isn't in it. GEORGE is now wearing a jacket to match his trousers, and a tie. He has a flower behind his ear, too. Drink has, if anything made him more morose. SHIRLEY is a slightly plainer girl than JENNIFER, about the same age. She is thinner, with dark hair and round, dark tinted spectacles. A depressive, during the whole of the following, she wears an expression of doom.)*

GEORGE. (*Without enthusiasm.*) Aye, aye, conga ... Hic! Aye, aye, conga. Aye ... Hic! Aye, conga ... (*To HUMPHREY.*) I feel daft, doin' this. Can I ... hic! stop now?

(*HUMPHREY breaks off his embrace with JENNIFER and starts to organize everybody. Sits SHIRLEY on the settee. JENNIFER puts her handbag on the floor, DS of armchair.*)

HUMPHREY. Yes, yes, yes, yes. Sit down, girls. I'll get the glasses! Glasses, George!

JENNIFER. (*Sits on settee beside SHIRLEY.*) Oh, I like champagne! Specially with orange juice! (*Starts to check her make-up.*) You got any orange juice?

GEORGE. I dunno ... Humphrey! Humphrey, can I have ... hic! ... can I have a word? (*He leads HUMPHREY downstage right, clutching his arm. An urgent stage whisper.*)

HUMPHREY. What?

GEORGE. Why ... er ... why didn't you take 'em back to your place?

HUMPHREY. This is *nearer*, George. Besides, what about Consuela ... biggest mouth in Spain!

GEORGE. Yes, but ... hic (*Waves gaily at girls to keep them quiet.*) ... couldn't you have gone back to *their* place?

HUMPHREY. Psychology! Make 'em play away from home, you're more likely to score!

GEORGE. I don't want to score! 'Specially not with wossname ... hic ... she's been a misery all evening.

HUMPHREY. You make a lovely couple, George. Get the glasses!

(*He breaks away from GEORGE, crosses and sits between the girls on the settee. Starts to take the foil off the champagne bottle. Grumbling, GEORGE goes to the sideboard, starts to hunt out a selection of assorted glasses.*)

WHEN THE CAT'S AWAY

HUMPHREY. (*To JENNIFER.*) Well, well, well ... nice glass of champagne, eh, love? A few laughs ... (*Turns to SHIRLEY.*) A few laughs ... (*Sees her glum face.*) Oh, god. (*Back to JENNIFER.*) Y'know, it's been over a week since we had a good ... meal ... together. Let's make the most of ... of ... of ...

(*He is distracted as SHIRLEY abruptly stands, crosses round the back of the settee and over to GEORGE at the sideboard. HUMPHREY and JENNIFER watch her, puzzled. SHIRLEY comes up behind GEORGE and whispers in his ear. He jumps, startled.*)

GEORGE. Nyaa! W-what? (*Indicates W.C.*) Oh, it's in there.

(*SHIRLEY crosses and enters the W.C., closing the door. GEORGE brings the assorted glasses over and sits in the armchair. JENNIFER leans forward, indicating towards W.C.*)

JENNIFER. (*Concerned.*) Did she say what she wanted to do?
GEORGE. Er ... not in detail, no ... hic.
JENNIFER. Is there anything in there she can harm herself with?
GEORGE. Well, there's the Royal Jubilee lavatory brush, but I don't ... hic! ... How d'you mean, "Harm herself?"

HUMPHREY. She's been a bit ... depressed lately, George.

JENNIFER. Her boyfriend's been unfaithful to her ... after four years ... went back to his wife.

HUMPHREY. Still, we mustn't let it spoil our...

GEORGE. (*Alarmed.*) Hang on! (*Stands.*) She's not likely to do anything stupid, is she? Hic. I've just decorated in there!

HUMPHREY. No, no. It's all talk,

JENNIFER. She might. (*Stands.*) Yesterday she threatened to jump out of the window.

HUMPHREY. (*Standing.*) You live in a basement.

JENNIFER. That's why I didn't take it too seriously ... but she had the thought! (*To GEORGE.*) Is there anything *else* in there?

GEORGE. No. Well ... there's a packet o' Bile Beans ... but nobody would *choose* to go that way, would they?

JENNIFER. I just don't think she should be alone in there. (*The two men look at each other.*)

HUMPHREY. Aye, well, er ...

GEORGE. (*Hurries to the W.C.*) She's right, Humphrey! I'd better have a quick look and make sure that she's ... (*He kneels to peer through the keyhole, as the door opens inwards and SHIRLEY emerges. She looks down at GEORGE and sniffs.*) Ah ... er ... I was just ... ah ...(*SHIRLEY looks at him stonily, sniffs, then crosses to the settee and sits. GEORGE follows her.*) ... I was just going to fasten my shoelace ... (*Lifts a foot to illustrate.*) Ah ... and then I realized I was wearing slip-on casuals ... so I won't bother.

HUMPHREY. One good thing. It's got rid of your hiccups.

(*He chuckles. JENNIFER joins in, rather relieved. They all sit, with GEORGE on the armchair, JENNIFER, HUMPHREY and SHIRLEY on the settee [JENNIFER and HUMPHREY between GEORGE and SHIRLEY]. HUMPHREY determined not to let the evening sag.*)

HUMPHREY. Right ... come on, George. Get the bottle open! Let's cheer ourselves up ... (*Arm 'round JENNIFER.*) ... We'll put a bit of music on in a minute ... (*To SHIRLEY.*) You'll like that, won't you, Shirley? (*Looks at her, then back to JENNIFER.*) She'll like that. Well, well, well ... this is nice.

GEORGE. (*Wrestling with champagne cork, wire, etc.*) Seen any good films lately?

JENNIFER. What?

GEORGE. Films ... umph ... seen any good ones lately? Umph ...!

JENNIFER. Oh, yes. Saw one on Monday, didn't we Shirley? (*SHIRLEY makes an effort, smiles wanly.*) It was very funny ... with Tatum O'Neal.

HUMPHREY. Who?

JENNIFER. Tatum O'Neal ... (*HUMPHREY looks blank.*) Film star! (*A thought.*) Sort of ... a younger Zasu Pitts.

HUMPHREY. Oh, yes! Very good!

GEORGE. (*Still trying to pull the cork.*) I watch the telly, meself ... umph ... Good program on last week ... all about sewage. D'you know when you drink a glass of water, it's been through an average of seventeen kidneys before ...

HUMPHREY. George! Do you mind? Give me that bottle. (*He reaches across and plucks the cork out with ease.*)

GEORGE. Yes ... well, I'd loosened it, hadn't I? (*HUMPHREY pours out the drinks into assorted glasses.*) Not too much for me, Humphrey. It gives me the runs.

HUMPHREY. (*Distaste.*) Yes, George.

GEORGE. (*To JENNIFER.*) Last time I drank champagne, I was in and out o'bed like a yo-yo ...

HUMPHREY. *Yes*, George! Can we ... you know ... talk about something else?

GEORGE. Beer, on the other hand, goes straight through me. In one end and ...

HUMPHREY. For pity's sake, Geo ... Have you any orange juice?

GEORGE. No. There's a couple of oranges in the kitchen.

JENNIFER. (*Stands.*) I'll do it.

WHEN THE CAT'S AWAY 63

HUMPHREY. (*Stands.*) I'll come with you. (*Escorts her towards the kitchen.*) Give you a hand to squeeze 'em! (*Sexy chuckle.*)

JENNIFER. (*Giggles.*) Ohoo ...

GEORGE. (*Half standing.*) Humphrey ... don't leave me with wossname ... I'll show you where they are.

HUMPHREY. (*Firmly waving him down.*) I'll find 'em, George! Don't worry.

(*He and JENNIFER exit to the kitchen. GEORGE reluctantly settles back in the armchair, fidgets, clears throat, crosses legs, smiles weakly at SHIRLEY, looks at watch.*)

GEORGE. Er ... it's ... um ... it's getting late. Hehehe ...

SHIRLEY. (*Looks over at him intensely. Removes her tinted spectacles. Puts them on the coffee table.*) I'm not going to bed with you, you know! (*Drinks her drink.*)

GEORGE. (*Electrified with alarm.*) No! No ... yes. Right. No.

SHIRLEY. (*With intensity, moving along the settee towards GEORGE.*) I know what men think of me. They think I'm anybody's.

GEORGE. No, no. Not at all. Perish the thought. (*Strangled cry towards kitchen.*) Humphrey!

SHIRLEY. When you give yourself to a man, he loses respect for you ... and leaves you.

GEORGE. Oh, definitely, yes! Yes. What d'you think of the Muppets?

SHIRLEY. And if you don't, they think you're frigid.

GEORGE. That Kermit the frog ... you have to laugh ...

SHIRLEY. I'm not frigid ... (*Puts her hand on his knee.*)

GEORGE. (*Leaps out of his armchair and backs away 'round the settee. She remains seated.*) I ... er ... I ... I ... I ...

SHIRLEY. It's just that one more rejection will finish me.

GEORGE. Very likely. (*Deep voice.*) Don't risk it!

SHIRLEY. All I ask for is a little understanding ...

GEORGE. I don't understand.

SHIRLEY. (*Trying to pull herself together.*) I'm sorry. I'm ... I'm embarrassing you. I didn't want to embarrass you. I do tend to become hyper-emotional in inter-communicating situations. (*A sob.*) I quite like Fozzie Bear.

GEORGE. What?

SHIRLEY. Fozzie Bear.

GEORGE. Oh, yeah! He's good, Fozzie. Yes. You have to laugh.

SHIRLEY. I do like a man with a sense of humor.

GEORGE. Yeah ... (*Uneasy.*) I don't laugh *that* much. Just a bit.

SHIRLEY. You're trying to cheer me up.

GEORGE. No, no. I'm not. Honest.

SHIRLEY. You're a kind man. I could give myself to a kind man.

GEORGE. Omygod! Look, erm ... it's nothing *personal,* but, y'see ... I'm not a very *physical* sort of ... of ... I'm, erm, well, that side of things ... *doing* things ... it's ... I'm not *against* it ... now and then ... but, I'm perhaps less ... interested ... in it than ... than ... than ... some people who are more interested in it than I am. (*Sees she's listening sympathetically, gains confidence and gradually joins her on the settee.*) There's nothing wrong with me. I mean, I've got all the ... it's just that ... well, there are so many *other* things in my life. Things like ... erm ... (*Can't think of one.*) ... erm ... So there you are. It's nothing personal.

SHIRLEY. I think I understand.

GEORGE. (*Relieved.*) Oh, good. (*Picks up a drink.*)

SHIRLEY. (*Gripping his knee.*) You need my help!

GEORGE. No! I ... (*Terrified, he rears back and accidentally spills his drink down the front of her dress.*) Oh! I'm sorry ... sorry ... (*He ineffectually wipes the front of her dress with his hands. She stiffens with pleasure.*)

SHIRLEY. Mmmm ...

GEORGE. I didn't mean to ... oh, dear.

(*HUMPHREY and JENNIFER enter from the kitchen. He carries a small jug of orange juice. HUMPHREY looks at GEORGE, who is still dabbing at SHIRLEY's dress.*)

HUMPHREY. (*Surprised, not knowing.*) Hullo, hullo ... these two didn't waste much time!

GEORGE. No, no. I'm not ... I didn't ... (*Realizes what he's doing, snatches his hands away.*)

SHIRLEY. (*Stands.*) Accidents will happen. I'll have to take my dress off. (*Lifts her dress up over her head.*)

GEORGE. Don't do that! (*Drops to his knees and pulls it down.*)

HUMPHREY. (*Amused.*) She's soaked through. You take it off, love. (*She goes to remove it. GEORGE stops her again.*)

GEORGE. Not here! Use ... use the bathroom. (*Indicates bathroom.*) You can dry it on the radiator.

SHIRLEY. Thank you. It was my fault. It's always my fault. (*She starts up the stairs.*)

(*JENNIFER grips HUMPHREY's arm.*)

JENNIFER. (*Stage whisper.*) She can't go to the bathroom on her own! Not in that mood!

HUMPHREY. What? Oh, yes ... (*Indicates .*) George.

GEORGE. Oh, no, no, no. Not me.

HUMPHREY. *(To JENNIFER.)* What's she gonna do? Beat herself to death with his rubber duck?

JENNIFER. There's all sorts in a bathroom ... *(Calls after SHIRLEY.)* Shirley ... *(Starts up the stairs after her.)* I'll help you.

SHIRLEY. I'll be all right.

JENNIFER. No, I'll help you. *(Scowls at HUMPHREY.)* Men! *(To SHIRLEY.)* It won't stain if we sponge it quickly ... *(They exit to the bathroom, closing the door.)*

HUMPHREY. *(Sour.)* You've excelled yourself tonight, you have.

GEORGE. Eh?

HUMPHREY. Pull yourself together! Dim the lights ... I'll put on some romantic music ... let's try and save what's left of the evening! *(He crosses to the sideboard and begins to sort through the records.)*

GEORGE. Humphrey, I really don't want to get involved in this sort of ...

HUMPHREY. Dim the lights!

GEORGE. Yes. *(He clicks out the table lamp on the sideboard, leaving that corner of the room in shadow.)* I still don't ...

HUMPHREY. Not *that* one, George. I can't see what I'm doing.

(GEORGE clicks the lamp back on, then crosses to the front door and turns off one of the lights from a wall switch. The lighting is now more

subdued and romantic. During this. HUMPHREY looks through the records.)

GEORGE. Sorry ...

HUMPHREY. "Vera Lynn at the El Alamein Reunion." *(Puts it aside.)* "Blaze Away with the Munn and Feltons Footwear Brass Band."

GEORGE. It's a good one, that.

HUMPHREY. *(Looks at him sourly.)* Lays it aside.) Haven't you got anything ... Ah! This'll do! *(He puts on some soft, smoochy, music, low. GEORGE joins him.)*

GEORGE. I've changed me mind. Let's just give 'em a cup o' cocoa and they can go home, eh?

HUMPHREY. No, no, no. *(Leads GEORGE downstage.)* In a couple of minutes they'll be back down ... there'll be romantic music ... there'll be more champagne ... open the other bottle ...

GEORGE. But ...

HUMPHREY. Open the bottle! *(GEORGE reluctantly begins to open the second bottle.)* And there'll be me ... and there'll be you ... and this time, *nothing* is going to go wrong!

(Behind them, the bedroom door opens and MILDRED appears, pulling on her frilly negligee over night attire. She looks sleepy. ETHEL is just behind her, also in a negligee.)

MILDRED. George? What's going on?

WHEN THE CAT'S AWAY 69

(GEORGE and HUMPHREY freeze, stricken. The champagne cork pops. HUMPHREY snatches the flower from his ear and flings it through the open kitchen hatch. GEORGE goes to do the same, a split second later but the hatch slams down and his flower bounces off it. MILDRED sweeps down the stairs, followed by ETHEL. ETHEL is yawning.)

MILDRED. What *are* you two playing at? Records at this time of night? How do you expect us to sleep?
GEORGE. *(Dithering.)* Ah ... I ... uh ... er ... *(Terrified whinny as he indicates ETHEL and MILDRED to HUMPHREY.)*
HUMPHREY. *(Quicker on his feet.)* Ah .. they're here, then, George. They're not in France. Ahaha ...

(MILDRED crosses to the record player and switches it off.)

ETHEL. There was a strike of baggage loaders. We weren't allowed on the plane.
HUMPHREY. No, you wouldn't be.
MILDRED. Wasted the whole afternoon. We were back here by seven o'clock and ... Champagne?
HUMPHREY. Yes ...
GEORGE. Yes ...
HUMPHREY. ... it's for *you.*

GEORGE. Eh?

HUMPHREY. We heard about the strike ... on the radio ... didn't we, George?

GEORGE. Oh, yeah! Yeah!

HUMPHREY. ... and we thought ... the girls will need cheering up ... and so ... (*Gestures.*) *champagne!*

GEORGE. Yes! It's all ready! We've got the glasses out and ... and ... (*Sees SHIRLEY's round, tinted spectacles on the coffee table. Picks them up and puts them on.*) ... the glasses ... and everything ...

(*MILDRED gazes at him, baffled.*)

ETHEL. (*Suspicious.*) So where have you been all evening?

HUMPHREY. Erm ... that's a fair question, George.

GEORGE. Oh, very fair. Very fair. We ... we ... we've been to the pictures!

HUMPHREY. Right ... good film. With that ... uh ... Tatum O'Neal.

ETHEL. Who?

GEORGE. Tatum O'Neal ... big chap ... moustache ...

MILDRED. They're not your glasses, George.

GEORGE. Aren't they? (*Takes them off. Looks at them.*) Oh, no ... you're right, they're not. They're yours, Humphrey. (*Thrusts them at him.*)

HUMPHREY. Thank you, George. (*Puts them on.*) Thank *you*. So, shall we ... (*Takes them off and tucks them in his pocket.*) Shall we celebrate the safe return of our loved ones? (*Picks up a glass.*) It's already poured, so we'll ...

ETHEL. Humphrey ... it's after midnight.

MILDRED. (*Picking up a glass, brightly.*) That's the only time to drink champagne!

(*She sits on the settee. ETHEL eventually sits beside her. HUMPHREY sits in the armchair. GEORGE hovers behind the settee, glancing up nervously at the bathroom, pointing at the door, as though HUMPHREY might have forgotten their problem.*)

MILDRED. *I* think its very nice of Humphrey and George to surprise us like this ...

ETHEL. (*Thawing.*) Well ...

MILDRED. The occasional little surprise can help a marriage.

HUMPHREY. If it's the right sort. Yes.

MILDRED. I've said to George, many a time ... (*She turns and sees him pointing frantically at the bathroom*)

GEORGE. Ah ... "Bang! Bang!" They went ... (*Mimes shooting revolver with his finger.*) ... and the cowboy fell out ... of the window ... of the saloon ... this Tatum O'Neal feller ... good film.

HUMPHREY. (*Hastily.*) Good film. So, what flight are you actually ... (*Dropping his hand, he feels the handbag beside the armchair, looks stricken.*) ... er ... ah ... catching, then?

ETHEL. They've booked us on Monday ... ten o'clock.

GEORGE. (*Squeaky.*) Not 'til Monday? (*Deep voice.*) Not 'til Monday.

(*The two WOMEN turn to look at him. HUMPHREY quickly holds up the handbag and indicates it to GEORGE, then hastily puts it out of sight again.*)

GEORGE. Hardly worth comin' back here. You could have waited at the ... (*Sees handbag.*) Nyaa!

ETHEL. Always assuming the strike is over.

(*GEORGE comes 'round the back of HUMPHREY's chair. During the following, he hooks his foot through the strap of the handbag and back behind the settee, dragging the handbag with him.*)

HUMPHREY. Ah, it might be over *now*, y'see. These things can end just like that ... (*Tries to click his fingers, but they are too damp to click. He wipes then on his trousers and finally clicks them.*) that. So why not pop back to the airport and see if ...)

ETHEL. Don't be ridiculous, Humphrey.

HUMPHREY. It was just a thought, love. I'm as disappointed as you, believe me. I know you were looking forward to this holiday ... and then this thing coming up ... the strike of the handbag handlers ... and, er ... well ... I know that George is as disappointed as I am ... for you.

(*MILDRED turns to look at GEORGE, just as he reaches the corner of the settee. He swivels his leg out of sight behind the settee, just in time. He beams at her. She turns back to HUMPHREY. GEORGE stoops to pick up the handbag disappearing from sight.*)

MILDRED. Yes, but ... (*Turning back to GEORGE.*) Oh, well, he ... (*Can't see him.*) George?

GEORGE. (*Pops his head up over the top of the settee, startling both MILDRED and ETHEL.*) Yes, my love?

MILDRED. Stop dancing about. Come and sit with us.

GEORGE. (*Stands, hands behind his back.*) Yes, I will ... (*Backs towards W.C.*) In a minute. I ... just want to ... to ... to go to, er ... it's the champagne.

MILDRED. You haven't had any.

GEORGE. No. But it's the *thought* of the champagne.

HUMPHREY. *(To distract them.)* The thing is, ladies ... look at me when I'm talking to you ... hahaha ... George and I ...

(MILDRED and ETHEL turn back to HUMPHREY. GEORGE seizes the opportunity and throws the handbag into the W.C. and closes the door. Then hesitates, uncertain whether to come back or not. He creeps up to the bathroom, tries the door. It's locked. He creeps down again, during the following.)

HUMPHREY. ... we realized, as soon as you'd gone out of the door, we realized that ... er ... we were alone. And that we missed you. Yes. Absence makes the heart grow fonder, as they say...

ETHEL. We've only been gone a few hours.

HUMPHREY. A few hours can be a lifetime, Ethel. Parting is such sweet sorrow ... but ... two's company ... and love is a many splendored thing.

ETHEL. Humphrey, we'll have none of your dirty talk.

HUMPHREY. It's just that ... you were meant for me and I was meant for ...

(During the above, GEORGE makes a decision. He opens and closes the W.C. door and heads back towards them, zipping up his trousers.)

HUMPHREY. ... Ah! You're back, George!

MILDRED. That was quick.

GEORGE. Ah ... uh ... false alarm. How would it be if we all went for a nice walk?

MILDRED. Sit down! (*He does, beside her.*) Pour some more champagne.

ETHEL. Not for me, thank you. I've got a slight headache.

MILDRED. (*Standing.*) I'll get you an aspirin. There's some in the bathroom.

GEORGE. No!

HUMPHREY. (*Standing.*) No! I'll get them!

GEORGE. Humphrey'll get them! They're ... they're a bit heavy for a woman.

MILDRED. Don't be silly ... (*Prepares to go.*)

HUMPHREY. (*Stopping her.*) Ah ... you've had a tiring day, Mildred. Save your legs.

MILDRED. Oh, well ... You know where they are, George. (*Indicates bathroom.*)

GEORGE. Eh?

MILDRED. In the cabinet, next to your "Odor-Eaters."

GEORGE. Oh, yes ... (*Hesitantly starts up stairs.*)

HUMPHREY. (*With great meaning.*) Check that the cap on the bottle is tight. Make sure they don't come out!

GEORGE. What? Oh, yes! Right!

MILDRED. Bring two ... I'll get a glass of water.

GEORGE. Ah ... right.

(*MILDRED goes to exit to the kitchen, as GEORGE reaches the bathroom door. It opens. SHIRLEY comes out in bra and pants, about to say something. GEORGE pushes her back into the bathroom and follows her in, closing the door. At the same time, HUMPHREY pushes MILDRED into the kitchen, then turns to ETHEL, mopping his brow.*)

HUMPHREY. (*To ETHEL.*) Well, now ... I'm sorry about your headache, love. I blame myself ... I've been a rotten husband ...
ETHEL. Yes.
HUMPHREY. Why don't you come home with me ... right this minute ... and I'll try and make it up to you.
ETHEL. It's after midnight!
HUMPHREY. What better time? New day ... new start. (*Glances up towards bathroom, uneasy.*) I've got the car, we could leave at once.
ETHEL. (*Sour.*) Humphrey ...
HUMPHREY. Consuela's missing you. You're the only one with a smattering of Spanish. There's a limit to what I can do with blows and curses ...
ETHEL. It's no use ...
HUMPHREY. Your Harrod's catalogue arrived yesterday ... there's a sable coat on the cover ... that might have been made for you.

WHEN THE CAT'S AWAY

ETHEL. Are you trying to *bribe* me to come home?

HUMPHREY. Yes!

ETHEL. It won't work. (*A beat.*) Were the sleeves full, or three quarter?

HUMPHREY. Both. You'd look lovely in it. So why don't we just ... ?

ETHEL. I'm not packed. I'm not even dressed.

HUMPHREY. Leave it to me! (*He bounds up the stairs as MILDRED comes in from the kitchen with a glass of water.*)

ETHEL. Humphrey, I haven't said that I'll ... Humphrey!

HUMPHREY. And there's a hat to go with it! (*Exits to bedroom.*)

ETHEL. Humphrey ... Tch! (*To MILDRED.*) He wants to take me home with him ... Now!

MILDRED. (*Knowing.*) Oh, yes?

ETHEL. I don't know what's got into him.

MILDRED. Don't you? (*Arch.*) He has been without your ... home cooking ... for a week.

ETHEL. But I don't do any home ... (*Dreadful thought.*) Oh, *that!*

MILDRED. Exactly. A man can get a little restless ...

(*HUMPHREY hurtles from the bedroom, stuffing clothes into ETHEL's half open suitcase. He's got her coat slung over his shoulder. He hurries downstairs, dropping clothes, trampling over them, etc.)*

HUMPHREY. No point in hanging about, getting dressed ... I mean, you'll only have to get undressed the other end, so you might as well ...

ETHEL. Just a moment ...

HUMPHREY. (*He drops her suitcase and puts her coat 'round her shoulders.*) Yes, love? (*Glances towards bathroom*)

ETHEL. *If* I come home ... now ... do you have anything ... physical in mind?

HUMPHREY. I don't quite ... (*Realizes.*) Oh ... dear me, no. I've gone right off that sort of thing. It's more trouble than it's worth.

ETHEL. (*Mixed feelings.*) Oh ...

MILDRED. I knew I shouldn't have left him alone with George.

HUMPHREY. (*To MILDRED.*) So, if you'll excuse us ...

ETHEL. Just a moment. What about you and this ... Jennifer.

HUMPHREY. Ah ...

ETHEL. ... how close *are* you?

HUMPHREY. Erm ... look, love. I will put as much distance between me and her as I can. How's that? (*Stage whisper.*) I'll sack her!

ETHEL. (*Mollified.*) Well, all right ... (*Turns to MILDRED.*) Mildred, you've been a tower of strength to me ...

MILDRED. We're all family ...

(The SISTERS embrace. HUMPHREY fidgets. GEORGE comes from the bathroom, closing the door. He looks relieved, carries a bottle of aspirin.)

GEORGE. *(Heading downstairs.)* I got them. I got the aspirins ... so we're all right ... for the moment, eh, Humphrey? Hehehe ... *(Takes the scene in.)* What ... what're you doing?
MILDRED. Humphrey's taking Ethel home. Isn't it nice?
GEORGE. *(Can hardly believe it.)* What, *now?!* Oh, no, no, no no ... you can't *do* that, Humphrey! You can't leave me here alone with-with-with ... Mildred!
HUMPHREY. You'll manage, George.
GEORGE. No, I won't, no! Y'see, I ... I ... *(To ETHEL.)* Take me with you!
MILDRED. What's the matter? You're shaking like a leaf.
GEORGE. *(Babbles.)* I'm ... a ... look, I, I, I ... we ... we ... we ... let's *both* go with them! It'll be company in the car!
MILDRED. George ...
GEORGE. I'm not letting him go ... not now! He'll be out of it ... and I'll be in it. The house, I mean ...
HUMPHREY. *(Shakes his hand warmly.)* I want you to know that I appreciate all you've done for Ethel. If I can every do anything in return ...

GEORGE. You can stay here!

HUMPHREY. ... don't hesitate to ask. G'night, Mildred. C'mon, Ethel ...

ETHEL. B-but I ... don't *push!* (*He picks up her suitcase and hurries her out of the front door. MILDRED beams after them.*)

GEORGE. (*Despairing.*) He can't just go like that ... he can't, he can't. He can't do it, Mildred. He can't go ...

MILDRED. He's gone. (*She closes the front door.*)

GEORGE. (*A whimper.*) Oh ... oh ... (*Takes a couple of aspirin.*)

MILDRED. And Ethel's gone, too. So we're back to normal.

GEORGE. Um ...

MILDRED. And I'll tell you another thing ... (*She sits on settee.*)

GEORGE. What?

MILDRED. It means you can come to France with me, after all.

GEORGE. (*Dismayed.*) Oh, gawd ... (*Inspired thought.*) Good idea! I'll get our coats!

MILDRED. Not *now!* Monday. Impatient boy. (*Chuckles and pats settee beside her.*) Sit here ... we'll finish off the champagne .. together ... alone.

GEORGE. Well, all right, but ... (*Goes to sit.*) Ah! No ... I know you ... you're in one of your moods. If ... if I sit here there'll be limbs flyin' everywhere. It'll end in chaos!

MILDRED. George, we're married ... and it's been weeks since we had any chaos.

GEORGE. (*Reluctantly sits.*) Yes, but ... y'see ... er ... I'm not against the idea, Mildred ... there's nothing I'd like *more* but ... it ... it's the champagne. It goes straight to me faculties.

MILDRED. You've only had a tiny little drop.

GEORGE. Oh, it's enough.

MILDRED. (*Long-suffering.*) Yes, it would be. D'you think a cup of strong black coffee would help?

GEORGE. I doubt it very ... Yes! It might! You go in there and make one, my sweet. (*Helps her up, steers her towards the kitchen.*) Take your time ... I'll ... I'll sit here and ... uh ... prepare meself mentally.

MILDRED. Well, don't overdo it! (*Exits to kitchen.*)

GEORGE. No ... Phew ... (*He hurries across the room and starts up the stairs as the bathroom door opens and JENNIFER comes out. They meet each other on the stairs. JENNIFER is carrying SHIRLEY's dress.*)

JENNIFER. It's still stained. Have you got any cleaning fluid?

GEORGE. Keep your voice down ... my wife ... (*Indicates kitchen.*)

(*JENNIFER sweeps past him, looks for her handbag beside the armchair. GEORGE follows her, agitated, keeping one eye on the kitchen door.)*

GEORGE. Look ... look, Humphrey's gone home. So why don't you and your friend just leave quietly and ...
JENNIFER. We will, don't you worry! I'll phone for a taxi ...
GEORGE. No, no, I'll do it! (*Picks up phone.*) You go back ...
JENNIFER. Where's my handbag? (*She drapes the dress over the back of the settee.*)
GEORGE. What? (*Dials.*) Oh, it's in the ... in the wossname. (*Indicates.*) The loo.
JENNIFER. What's it doing there? (*Crosses to W.C.*)
GEORGE. I threw it in ...
JENNIFER. Huh! (*Exits to W.C. reappears with the handbag.*) It's all wet!
GEORGE. Eh? Oh, sorry about that ... I just ... (*To phone.*) Hullo? Hampton Wick Minicabs? I'd like to ...
MILDRED. (*Off.*) George ...
GEORGE. (*To phone.*) Hang on ... (*Lays phone aside, hurries across to W.C. To JENNIFER.*) Please ... just stay in there for a couple o' minutes. Have a look at the Royal Jubilee lavatory brush! (*Pushes JENNIFER in, closes door. Calls to kitchen.*) Yes, my love?

MILDRED. (*The hatch opens. MILDRED calls through.*) Would you like a sponge finger with it?

GEORGE. With what? Oh, yes! Yes, good idea. (*She closes the hatch. He hurries back to the telephone. Picks it up. To phone.*) Hullo? Yes ... I'd like to order a cab ... um? (*Opens front door to check the number.*) Forty-six, Peacock Crescent ... yes. Right away, please. My name? Why d'you want my name? Oh ... I see ... Tatum O'Coleman ... yes.

(*MILDRED comes from the kitchen carrying a tray with cups of coffee and a plate of sponge fingers. GEORGE becomes aware of her.*)

GEORGE. Thank you ... (*Phone down. He turns to MILDRED. Points at phone.*) Er ... uh ... it ... it was the speaking clock.

MILDRED. Oh, what *is* the time?

GEORGE. Uh ... I forgot to ask. (*Looks at tray.*) What's this?

MILDRED. Black coffee and sponge fingers.

GEORGE. At this time o' night? No, no, no, no. (*Takes tray from her. Puts it down.*) It'll give us indigestion. Ridiculous idea. No, the best thing we can do is go straight up to ... (*During the above, MILDRED has seen the dress draped on the settee. She picks it up and holds it at arms length. GEORGE turns and sees her.*) ... ah.

MILDRED. Whose dress is this?

GEORGE. Er ... (*Dithers.*) ... mine!

MILDRED. What? Oh, George ...

GEORGE. No, I bought it. For you. This afternoon.

MILDRED. You ... bought me a dress?

GEORGE. Yes! See? There it is! (*Takes it from her.*) Haha ... erm ... it was a going-away present, but you'd already gone.

MILDRED. (*Fingers the material.*) Oh, it's ... it's lovely. It's not quite my size but ...

GEORGE. (*Rolls the dress up, prepared to throw it away.*) Oh, good. We'll ...

MILDRED. No, George ... no! (*Takes it from him.*) I'm sure I can alter it ... oh, you can be *so* sweet when you want to be.

GEORGE. Yes. Well ... (*Squares his shoulders.*) ... let us go straight up to bed, my precious.

MILDRED. (*Puzzled, but pleased.*) Bed?

GEORGE. (*He ushers her up the stairs. Arm 'round her waist.*) Strike while the iron is hot, so to speak. It's the champagne that's done it ...

MILDRED. I wish you'd make up your mind.

GEORGE. I have, I have! A man has ... needs, you know ... the urge comes over him to ... to *do* things.

MILDRED. I haven't seen you like this since England won the World Cup. (*She starts up the stairs.*)

GEORGE. Passion is roused, Mildred. I cannot wait another second. (*Takes dress from her.)* You will not need this with what I have in mind.

MILDRED. Oh, George.

GEORGE. *(Pausing outside bedroom door.)* So you go on in, I'll join you later.

MILDRED. *(Pausing on landing. Sour.)* I've heard that one before. What are you going to do? Sharpen your pencil collection again?

GEORGE. No ... this time I *will* come ... I just want to ... to ... go to the wossname.

MILDRED. I'll give you two minutes. And then I'm coming for you! *(Blows him an aggressive kiss and exits to the bedroom.)* One ... two ... three ... four ... five ... six ... seven.

GEORGE. *(Scurries to the bathroom, on the point of collapse. He opens the bathroom door, pulls SHIRLEY, still in bra and pants, out onto the landing.)* Quick ... come on out. *(SHIRLEY and GEORGE freeze as MILDRED sweeps from the bedroom, briskly winding an alarm clock.)*

MILDRED. ...fifteen ... sixteen ... seventeen ... eighteen ... nineteen ... *(She checks the alarm clock with the Grandmother clock on the landing, then adjusts the alarm clock.)* ... twenty ... twenty-one ... twenty-two ... twenty-three ... *(She exits to the bedroom, closing the door. During this move she has not seen the frozen tableau behind her.)*

GEORGE. *(Whimpers.)* Oh ...

SHIRLEY. (*Takes her dress from him and exits to the bathroom, closing the door.*) Tch! It's still damp!

GEORGE. (*To door.*) No! Look, I ... (*JENNIFER comes from the W.C. GEORGE sees her and hurries downstairs.*)

JENNIFER. I'm fed up ...

GEORGE. Nyaa ... Look, I've phoned for a taxi. Should be here in a minute. (*Ushers her towards the front door, opens it.*) Why don't you wait outside for it?

JENNIFER. Because it's cold ... and what about Shirley?

GEORGE. I'll sneak her out and all ... (*Attempts to push her out of the door.*)

MILDRED. (*Comes from the bedroom. Arch.*) ... forty-four ... forty-five ... forty- six ... George, I ... (*Takes in the scene.*)

GEORGE. Ah ...

MILDRED. (*Coming downstairs.*) And who is this?

GEORGE. Ah ... it's ... a woman, Mildred. She ... just knocked at the door. And ... (*To JENNIFER.*) We don't want any, thank you. Goodbye. (*Pushes her out and slams front door.*)

MILDRED. George ... don't be rude. (*Opens door, brings JENNIFER in.*) What can we do for you?

GEORGE. (*Hastily.*) She's ... she's selling flags.

MILDRED. At one o'clock in the morning?

WHEN THE CAT'S AWAY

GEORGE. Er ... it would seem so.

MILDRED. So where are they?

GEORGE. Ah ... she's sold 'em all. (*To JENNIFER.*) I can't think why you knocked, really.

JENNIFER. (*Closing front door firmly.*) I am not leaving until my taxi comes! (*She marches to center stage and folds her arms. GEORGE follows her, stricken.*)

GEORGE. Now look here, Jennifer, I've no wish to ... (*Hastily, to MILDRED.*) Assuming that is her name, of course ...

MILDRED. George, I am not a suspicious person by nature, but ...

GEORGE. (*Following the theory that attack is the best form of defense, rounds on her.*) How dare you! How dare you accuse me of ... of whatever it is you were going to. Is this all our marriage is worth? Do you, or do you not, trust me?

(*The bathroom door opens and SHIRLEY comes out, still in bra and pants, carefully holding her dress over her arm. She comes down the stairs.*)

SHIRLEY. I'm not staying in here any longer ... wife or no wife!

MILDRED. You were saying, George?

GEORGE. Er ...

JENNIFER. He's phoned for a taxi, Shirley.

SHIRLEY. About time. Give me a hand to get this on, will you?

(*During the following, JENNIFER helps SHIRLEY on with her dress, ad-libbing concern about the stain. GEORGE sinks into the armchair. Helps himself to a sponge finger. It's all been too much for him. Panic has given way to resignation. MILDRED leans on the armchair.*)

MILDRED. I'm listening.
GEORGE. I ... um ... (*A final throw.*) Who am I? Where is this place? Who are you?
MILDRED. On, come *on!* You can do better than that!
GEORGE. I don't think I can, Mildred. It was all Humphrey's idea. He wanted to bring 'em back. I didn't even want to go out with 'em in the first place!
JENNIFER. Oh, charming ...
SHIRLEY. All men are the same. You give them what they want then they reject you.
GEORGE. (*To MILDRED.*) She didn't. She didn't give me what I wanted! Honest.
MILDRED. But you did want it?
GEORGE. No! No, I didn't.
MILDRED. Suppose she ... (*Rage.*) ... She's putting my dress on!
GEORGE. Oh, gawd ...
SHIRLEY. It's mine!

JENNIFER. (*Amused.*) You'd never fill it, dear!

MILDRED. (*Turns on them, crosses to the front door, and opens it. Controlled rage.*) You. Out! And you ...

JENNIFER. But our taxi is ...

MILDRED. If you're going to do any waiting, you can wait outside. Now, out of my house, ... both of you!

(*A BEEP-BEEP of a taxi from outside.*)

JENNIFER. It's here, anyway. (*To GEORGE, who jumps.*) Men!

SHIRLEY. (*To GEORGE.*) I hope you're satisfied. I've got your fingermarks all down my chest!

MILDRED. Out!

(*The two GIRLS exit, on their dignity. MILDRED closes the front door. Tight lipped. She crosses to the settee in silence, struggling with her emotions. GEORGE eyes her uneasily, sitting like a little boy.*)

GEORGE. (*After several false starts.*) I ... I agree that it does *look* a bit suspicious ...

MILDRED. (*Sniffs emotionally.*)

GEORGE. ... but, I mean, you know me ... I'm not keen on that sort o' thing ... even at the best of times.

MILDRED. That's what I used to think. Now I realize it's just *me* you weren't keen on.

GEORGE. I wasn't keen on *them*, either. And they're young and attractive! What I mean is ... Come to bed, Mildred!

MILDRED. You think that'll solve everything, don't you?

GEORGE. It has crossed me mind, yes.

MILDRED. (*Musing. More in sorrow than in anger.*) Twenty-five years. Of you. Stirring your tea with your comb. Taking your teeth out in the cinema. Clipping the hair from your nostrils over my cold cream ...

GEORGE. I never claimed to be perfect.

MILDRED. Washing your personal parts with *my* flannel! Twenty-five years! (*Shakes her head in disbelief.*) And I've put up with it. And do you know why I've put up with it?

GEORGE. No. (*Genuinely interested.*) I've often wondered ...

MILDRED. *Because* ... (*Controls herself.*) ... because in some strange, twisted sort of way ... I was fond of you.

GEORGE. (*Gets up, crosses behind the settee and puts his hand on her shoulder.*) Well ... I'm ... I'm fond of you, Mildred. In some strange, twisted sort of way.

MILDRED. I feel dirty, George. (*Clutches his hand.*)

GEORGE. (*Indicating bedroom, hopefully.*) What, you mean you wanna ... er ... ?

MILDRED. No, I do not! Dear God ... have you no sensitivity at all?

GEORGE. (*Picking his nose, absentmindedly.*) 'Course I have, Mildred. That's not fair. I'm very sensitive ... Look, would it help if I didn't *take* me teeth to the cinema?

MILDRED. (*Shakes her head, mutely. As the front DOORBELL rings.*) If that is your ... bits of stuff ... coming back, you can go with them!

GEORGE. (*Crossing to open front door.*) They weren't mine! It was all Humphrey's fault. I had nothing to do with ... (*He opens the door. ETHEL sweeps in.*)

ETHEL. Oh, good! You haven't gone to bed yet!

MILDRED. Ethel?

ETHEL. Sorry about this. (*Starting up stairs.*) He rushed me off in such a hurry. I left all my make-up!

GEORGE. Where *is* Humphrey?

ETHEL. He's out in the car ... said he wouldn't come in. Didn't want to disturb you.

GEORGE. Oh, yes ...

ETHEL. If I hadn't insisted, he wouldn't have come back at all.

GEORGE. I believe you.

ETHEL. He's so thoughtful at times. (*Exits to bathroom.*)

GEORGE. Yes. (*To MILDRED.*) Now, then, he'll tell you. (*Calls out of front door.*) Humphrey! Yes ... I can see you. Why don't you come on in?

Humphrey! I can talk to you, or I can talk to Ethel! (*F/X car door SLAMMING.*) That's better ... come on. All the way. (*Crosses to MILDRED.*) It was nothing to do with me ... he'll tell you. (*Towards front door.*) Come in, Humphrey.

(*HUMPHREY appears at the front door, he looks shifty. Glances up at the bathroom door in wild speculation. He's twirling his car keys. He looks around the room uneasily, but doesn't come in any more than he needs to.*)

HUMPHREY. Ah ... hullo, George. Mildred. I won't stay ... don't want to disturb you ...

MILDRED. Come in, Humphrey. Close the door. (*He does so, reluctantly.*) George says you brought two young girls in here against his will.

HUMPHREY. (*Seemingly baffled.*) When was this?

GEORGE. Tonight.

HUMPHREY. What? Here? Well, where are they?

GEORGE. They've gone home ...

HUMPHREY. Ah ... (*Relaxes.*) So there's no ... proof ... of this.

MILDRED. I *saw* them!

HUMPHREY. You saw them? Um. (*To GEORGE.*) Oho, you're a deep one, George. (*To MILDRED.*) Fancy him having two women here all the time, without my knowing.

WHEN THE CAT'S AWAY

GEORGE. (*Stunned.*) No ... no! Stop messin' about ... *tell* her. Tell her I was against the whole thing!

(*During the following, ETHEL comes from the bathroom, sniffing back, suspicious. Starts down the stairs. She carries her big make-up case.*)

HUMPHREY. I'd like to help, George, but I don't know what you're talking about.

GEORGE. (*Impotent rage.*) The two girls you brought back here tonight! Wossname and ... Jennifer.

HUMPHREY. (*Innocent.*) Jennifer?

MILDRED. (*Firmly.*) Jennifer.

ETHEL. (*Aghast.*) Jennifer?!

HUMPHREY. Ah ... er ... You're just in time, love. It appears that he's been mucking about with my secretary. (*To GEORGE.*) You brute! (*To MILDRED.*) You have my deepest sympathy, Mildred ... (*To ETHEL.*) Shall we go?

ETHEL. Just a moment ...!

HUMPHREY. It's nothing to do with me if he hides a couple of girls in his bathroom ...

MILDRED. How did you know they were in the bathroom?

HUMPHREY. (*Thrown.*) Uh ... pass! (*To ETHEL.*) It's all fantasy, love. He's making it up.

MILDRED. I *saw* them. (*Stands.*)

GEORGE. (*Triumphant at being vindicated.*) She saw them! And one of 'em had her dress off! Yes. Hehehee (*Recalls himself as he sees MILDRED scowl.*) Shockin', shockin'.

ETHEL. (*Pokes HUMPHREY in the chest, indicating towards bathroom*) I knew it! I knew I could smell "Joy" in that bathroom!

HUMPHREY. That'll be Mildred's ...

ETHEL. Don't be ridiculous! She can't afford decent perfume!

MILDRED. Oh, thank you.

GEORGE. There's no "Joy" in this house, is there, Mildred?

MILDRED. Not a lot, George, no.

ETHEL. (*To HUMPHREY.*) No wonder you rushed me out, you ... you ... (*Snatches car keys.*) Give me those! I'm going home!

HUMPHREY. Ethel! Don't let's ... (*Slaps forehead in mock recollection.*) Just a minute! There *were* two girls ... yes, I remember now. They came to the door ... er ... erm ...

GEORGE. (*Helpfully.*) Sellin' flags?

HUMPHREY. Selling flags! Exactly!

GEORGE. At one o'clock in the morning?

(*HUMPHREY freezes, hating GEORGE. GEORGE chuckles.*)

HUMPHREY. (*To ETHEL, desperate.*) "The War Cry!" They were selling that! Jehovah's

Witnesses ... on the night shift ... (*Reaches for her.*)

ETHEL. Don't *touch* me! (*She exits through the front door.*)

HUMPHREY. Ethel ... (*He exits after her.*)

GEORGE. Hehehehe. Jehovah's Witnesses! Hehehee ...

MILDRED. (*Soberly to GEORGE.*) For a man facing death, you're remarkably cheerful. (*She closes the front door. GEORGE backs away.*)

GEORGE. Ah ... come on, Mildred ... can't you see he's guilty?

MILDRED. That doesn't mean you're innocent. Now, tell me the truth. Why *did* you bring that girl back?

GEORGE. Oh, gawd ... (*Dithers, frustrated, then decides he's got nothing to lose.*) All right ... I brought her back here to *do* things ... and we did ... five times ... ten! All over the place ... on the settee ... the stairs ... the kitchen table ... I even got your Royal place mats out and did it on *them!* So there ... I've confessed everything!

MILDRED. You're lying again!

GEORGE. All right! I plead innocent but insane!

MILDRED. George, you are not coming into my bed tonight ...

GEORGE. Thank you.

MILDRED. Move that table ... (*Starts to open the bed settee. The bed is already made up.*) I need time to ... get over your behavior. Perhaps in a week or two ...

GEORGE. (*Helpful.*) Make it a month, if you like, Mildred ... (*Fetches pillow from sideboard.*)

MILDRED. Ooh ... Give me a hand! (*He helps her open the bed settee.*)

GEORGE. What I mean is ... I tell you what ... I *will* come to France with you, how's that?

MILDRED. I don't think so. I'll go on my own. I'm sure I'll make one or two ... friends. Perhaps someone loafing about on the beach! I'll leave on Monday.

GEORGE. Yeah. Yeah ... you'll prob ... (*A thought.*) Hang on. Them beaches ... in France ... they're full o' young fellers ... bouncin' their ... an' flexin' their ... all bronzed an' hairy an' that ... (*Lays pillows down.*)

MILDRED. (*Provocative.*) Mmm ... I might be able to leave Sunday.

GEORGE. You wouldn't ...? (*The front DOORBELL rings. She moves to answer it.*) You wouldn't flirt with a froggie! They surrendered in 1940!

MILDRED. They might do it again in 1990! What's sauce for the goose, George ... (*She opens the front door. HUMPHREY enters, the fingers of his right hand stuffed in his mouth.*)

HUMPHREY. (*Mumbling incoherently.*) Unf ... unf ... ooh ... ung ...

MILDRED. Pardon?

HUMPHREY. (*Removing fingers from mouth, shaking hand in pain.*) She slammed the car door on me fingers!

MILDRED. (*Takes his hand and peers at it without too much sympathy.*) Oh, dear. That does look painful ... (*Blows on his fingers.*)

HUMPHREY. (*Agony.*) Ohoo!

GEORGE. Serves you right! *You* have cast a shadow over a very happy marriage.

MILDRED. Which one's that?

GEORGE. Ours!

MILDRED. Ah. I didn't recognize it from the description ...

HUMPHREY. She drove off like a maniac ... (*Examines fingers.*) Ooh ...

MILDRED. George will call you a taxi. He's good at that.

(*GEORGE looks guilty.*)

HUMPHREY. Thing is, y'see, she says she's gonna lock me out ... er ... She'll be over it by the morning, but ... er ... I was wondering ...? (*Gestures about.*)

GEORGE. Oh, no! No, no! We've only just got rid of "faceache" ... *he's* not stayin', Mildred!

MILDRED. (*Coldly.*) Why not? (*Indicates.*) He can share your bed.

GEORGE. Eh?

HUMPHREY. I'm not sure that I ...

MILDRED. (*To HUMPHREY.*) You won't know he's in there with you. I never have. (*Takes HUMPHREY's hand, examines fingers.*) George, get the sticking plaster.

GEORGE. It's not fair! He's the one who ...

MILDRED. Sticking plaster! (*GEORGE grumbles his way to the kitchen, exits. MILDRED crosses to the sideboard, rummages in a drawer and finds a tube of ointment.*) I've got some ointment here, somewhere. Not that you deserve it.

HUMPHREY. No ... (*Sits on the edge of the bed settee and clears his throat uneasily.*) Erm ... It's true, y'know ... what he told you.

MILDRED. Mmm?

HUMPHREY. It *was* all my idea ... those two girls ... He wanted nothing to do with 'em.

MILDRED. (*Crossing to sit beside him.*) Yes, that sounds more like the George I know.

HUMPHREY. So don't blame him, blame me, Mildred. It was all my fault. All of it.

MILDRED. (*Softening.*) It took a big man to admit it, Humphrey. (*Starts to smooth ointment on his fingers.*)

HUMPHREY. (*Self-deprecating.*) No ...

MILDRED. Yes, it did. But then, you *are* a big man. I've always suspected it.

HUMPHREY. My only excuse is, well ... I am a creature of strong passions ...

WHEN THE CAT'S AWAY 99

MILDRED. (*Breathing faster.*) I can tell that ... from your palm. Your love line goes right up your sleeve.

HUMPHREY. I know it's difficult for a woman to understand ...

MILDRED. Not at all.

HUMPHREY. Ethel ... she's never understood.

MILDRED. I understand ... what a lot of hair you have on your knuckles.

(*GEORGE enters from the kitchen. He holds a tin of sticking plasters. MILDRED lays down HUMPHREY's hand, reluctant.*)

GEORGE. We've only got a couple o' corn plasters ... and one o' them's been used.

HUMPHREY. I'll make do with the ointment. Thank you, Mildred.

MILDRED. My pleasure ... (*Stands and starts up the stairs.*)

GEORGE. It's a dead liberty, this is ... (*Sits on the edge of the bed settee and pulls his shoes off.*) I shouldn't be down here with him, I should be up there with you.

MILDRED. You're absolutely right, George.

GEORGE. Eh?

MILDRED. Humphrey's explained. So you're forgiven ... come to bed.

GEORGE. (*Uneasy.*) Ah ... er ... yes, but ... I got a headache, Mildred. Anyway, I can't leave him on his own, down here. He ... he's a guest. Perhaps tomorrow night?

MILDRED. Typical! (*Exits to bedroom.*)

GEORGE. (*Calling after her.*) I got a headache ... I have. Really. (*To HUMPHREY.*) I got a headache.

(*HUMPHREY starts to undress, folding his clothes over the armchair. GEORGE also starts to undress, dropping his clothes where they fall.*)

HUMPHREY. Tch, tch, tch! You should've gone with her, George. You were away, there.

GEORGE. How d'you mean?

HUMPHREY. Well, in my opinion, she was in the mood to ... (*Imitates GEORGE.*) ... *do* things.

GEORGE. She's always like that! There's hardly a month goes by without her gettin' restless! (*Confidentially.*) My private theory is, they put something in the dried egg during the war ...

HUMPHREY. They what?

GEORGE. To increase the population ... an' it's still affecting her.

HUMPHREY. You didn't like dried egg, then, George?

GEORGE. Never touched it.

HUMPHREY. Ah ...

GEORGE. It could've been in the snoek. I didn't like that, either.

HUMPHREY. No.

GEORGE. I'm makin' meself hungry ... (*Heads for kitchen.*) D'you fancy a cream cracker and a pickled onion?

HUMPHREY. (*With distaste.*) Not just now, thanks.

GEORGE. Um ... (*Exits to kitchen.*)

MILDRED. (*Appears from the bedroom carrying a pair of garish pyjamas in a cellophane wrapper.*) You can borrow a pair of ... (*Sees HUMPHREY's legs. Melts.*) My word ... George's pyjamas.

HUMPHREY. You're very kind, Mildred.

MILDRED. I bought them for Christmas ... (*She tosses them down.*) He's never worn them ...

HUMPHREY. No ... (*Examines them.*) They've got "Grrr" on the pocket.

MILDRED. "George Roland Roper" ... they're his initials.

HUMPHREY. Ah. Much obliged.

MILDRED. My pleasure. Good night, Humphrey.

HUMPHREY. Good night, Mildred. (*She exits to the bedroom, waggling her fingers, somewhat reluctant to go.*)

HUMPHREY. (*Unwraps the pyjamas. Looks at them with distaste.*) ... very nice.

(*GEORGE enters from the kitchen, carrying a jar of pickles and a packet of cream crackers. During the following, he and HUMPHREY finish undressing and get into their respective pyjamas. GEORGE's pyjamas are underneath the blankets of the made-up bed. He puts them on over his vest and underpants.*)

GEORGE. Mildred doesn't like me eatin' pickles and crackers in bed ... 'Cos they make me rumble.

HUMPHREY. Perhaps I *should* have tried to get a taxi ...

GEORGE. I was gonna have some gherkins as well, but that would have been unfair to you. I'm like Krakatoa after I've eaten Gherkins ... (*Pops a pickle into his mouth.*)

HUMPHREY. Have you any other irritating habits I should know about?

GEORGE. In bed? No, no. Well, there is one ... er ... but I don't do it every night. (*H e continues to get undressed. HUMPHREY pauses and waits for further information.*)

HUMPHREY. (*Eventually.*) What is it, George?

GEORGE. What's what? Oh ... It's when I'm restless and can't get to sleep ... I find it relaxes me, y'know ... (*Sees HUMPHREY has stopped undressing.*) Aren't you comin' to bed?

HUMPHREY. Not until you tell me what it is.

GEORGE. I sing myself to sleep.

HUMPHREY. You ... sing ... yourself ...?

GEORGE. To sleep ... yes. Nothing fancy, mind ... selections from "The Chocolate Soldier" ... "Oklahoma" ... that sort o' thing.

HUMPHREY. (*Flatly.*) "Oklahoma" ...

GEORGE. (*Climbing into bed.*) Unless you got any special requests? I could ...

HUMPHREY. (*Hastily.*) No, George, no! None at all! (*Crosses to turn off lights.*) I just want to get my head down. (*The room is now lit only by a STREET LIGHT from the front window. HUMPHREY climbs into bed beside GEORGE.*)

GEORGE. Right. Sure you wouldn't like a pickle?

HUMPHREY. No! Thank you ... Good night, George.

GEORGE. Good night, Humphrey. (*HUMPHREY settles down. GEORGE sighs and grunts for a few moments, then settles down with him. A long silence, then ... sings, quietly at first, then gathering volume.*) On the road to Mandal-ay-hay, where the flying' fishes play, an' the dawn comes up like thunder outer China 'cross the bay! On the road to ...

HUMPHREY. George!

GEORGE. Nyaa ...! (*Settles down again, pulling most of the bedclothes with him.*) Good night, Mildred!

CURTAIN

ACT II

Scene 2

AT RISE: The following morning, Sunday, about nine o'clock. Setting as before, with GEORGE and HUMPHREY seemingly snuggled down in an untidy bed. GEORGE snoring. A long ring at the DOORBELL. GEORGE stirs, then he sits up, coming out of a sleep.

GEORGE. (*Half awake.*) Stirrup pump! Man the stirrup pump! I ... what? Eh? Um? (*Looks around.*) Ah ... (*The DOORBELL rings again. He climbs out of bed, pulls on his old dressing gown and grunts his way to the front door.*) All right ... I'm comin'! (*He opens the front door. ETHEL steps inside, carrying a couple of suitcases. She's smartly dressed and still tight-lipped.*) Oh, mornin', Ethel.

ETHEL. Good morning.

GEORGE. I was dreamin' about ... (*Sees the suitcases, alarmed.*) Oh, no. I'm not havin' you back! I'll put up with one at a time ... (*Indicates bed.*) ... but not both of you!

ETHEL. These are Humphrey's clothes. And you can tell him I'm having the lock changed.

GEORGE. Oh, gawd ...

ETHEL. Until I've seen my solicitor, I'm holding his credit cards hostage. (*Turns to leave.*)

GEORGE. (*Restraining her.*) Ethel ... wait! Don't *leave* him here! You don't know what it's like, having to share a bed with him.

ETHEL. (*With distaste.*) I most certainly do.

GEORGE. Oh, yeah ... you would. But ... (*Tries another tack.*) ... he misses you, y'know. Something terrible. He was talkin' in his sleep last night ... "Darlin," he said ... "Darlin" ...

ETHEL. How do I know he was thinking of *me?*

GEORGE. Well, he wasn't thinkin' of *me!* One false move and I'd have stuck me pickle fork in him!

ETHEL. Knowing him, it wouldn't have saved you. (*Turns to leave again.*)

GEORGE. Wait! (*Restraining her.*) He's very upset, Ethel ... very restless. Tossing and turning, half the night. Really missing you, he was ... (*Moves to bed, taking her with him.*) He'll tell you himself ... Humphrey! Ethel's here! She ... (*He pulls back the bedclothes. HUMPHREY isn't there, just a jumble of pillows and bedclothes. Perhaps intended to give the effect of a body, perhaps accidental. ETHEL gazes at the pillows, her suspicious mind beginning to work. She continues to stare during the following. Unconcerned.*) Oh ... he's up already ... (*Crosses to the kitchen, still anxious only to get ETHEL and HUMPHREY to talk to each other.)* Prob'ly makin' a cup of ... Humphrey? Ethel's come to ... *(GEORGE goes into the kitchen, then comes out again. He crosses to the W.C. ETHEL slowly begins to look up from the bed, her suspicions hardening. She's ignoring GEORGE.)* You can't leave him here. Give him a chance ... Let the milk of human kindness gush forth over ... the porridge of suspicion and distrust ... *(Taps on the door of the W.C. The door swings open.)* Humphrey? *(Peers in.)* Oh ... He'll be in the bathroom ... *(Goes up the stairs to the bathroom. ETHEL slowly turns to look up at the bedroom door, her face hardening.)* I know in the past, he may have been a bit of a ... well, womanizer, I s'pose ... but I'm sure he wouldn't do it again. He's learned his lesson ... *(Looks into bathroom.)* Oh ... *(Comes downstairs, scratching his head, genuinely puzzled.)* Strange ... he's not in there, either. I can't understand it. *(He lifts the blankets again to make absolutely sure that HUMPHREY isn't in the bed. ETHEL continues to stare up at the bedroom, frozen.)* His clothes are still here and ... I dunno where he could possible ... *(Sees ETHEL's expression. Follows her gaze.)* ... where he could ... where ... *(They both gaze up at the bedroom door, then look at each other. GEORGE gestures to the bed, then himself, then upstairs, lost for words. Eventually.)* You don't ... you don't think ...? He wouldn't ... not with ... no. No, he wouldn't. Would he? *(ETHEL nods.)*

Would he? (*Thinks about it.*) He would! (*He and ETHEL turn towards the stairs as MILDRED comes from the bedroom. She wears a frilly negligee and looks bright and cheerful.*)

MILDRED. Good morning ... (*Slight surprise.*) Oh ... Ethel! How nice to see you, Ethel! And George! You're up already! (*She shuts the bedroom door and starts down the landing and stairs. ETHEL and GEORGE stay at the foot of the stairs, uncertain.*) Well, well, well ... Oh, I do like Sunday mornings! Don't you? The whole day ahead ... nothing to do. Heaven!

ETHEL. (*Coldly.*) Where is my husband?

MILDRED. *I* don't know. George, where's Humphrey?

GEORGE. (*Points.*) He's not in the kitchen ...

ETHEL. He's not in the bathroom.

GEORGE. He's not in the loo (*Points.*) and he's not down here! That only leaves one place he could be! (*Points to bedroom.*)

MILDRED. I don't quite ... (*Looks round at bedroom, then back at GEORGE. Outraged.*) What are you suggesting?

GEORGE. I am suggesting that ... that ... (*His nerve fails.*) I ... am ... (*To ETHEL.*) What are we suggesting, Ethel?

(*MILDRED is now at the bottom of the stairs, effectively blocking their way.*)

ETHEL. This whole matter can be cleared up quite simply. I just want to have a look in your bedroom, Mildred.

MILDRED. How dare you!

ETHEL. I sincerely hope I'm wrong. If you'll just step aside, I can ...

MILDRED. (*Folding her arms.*) I'm sorry. I think you should take my word for it.

GEORGE. Well, I don't!

MILDRED. (*To GEORGE.*) Very well, go and look. (*She steps aside and indicates the stairs.*)

GEORGE. (*Uncertain.*) Er ...

MILDRED. Go on.

GEORGE. Well ...

MILDRED. Go and look, George.

GEORGE. Right, I will. (*Goes to start up the stairs.*)

MILDRED. (*Suddenly barring his way with her arm.*) I see! Is this all our marriage is worth? Do you, or do you not trust me?

GEORGE. No, I don't.

MILDRED. So be it. (*Indicates stairs again.*) Let's go and look. Come on.

GEORGE. Right ...

MILDRED. (*At the top of the stairs, she stops, turns and bars his way again.*) *But* ... if you put one foot inside that door, things will never be the same between us. Any of us.

GEORGE. You mean he's in there?

WHEN THE CAT'S AWAY

(ETHEL starts up the stairs, pauses at the top, alongside MILDRED, anxious to be involved.)

MILDRED. If that's what you think, go ahead.
ETHEL. It is! Open the door, George.
GEORGE. I keep tryin' to!
MILDRED. Nobody's stopping you. *(Indicates door.)* Go on.
GEORGE. *(Gripping door handle.)* Right ...
MILDRED. *But ... (GEORGE pauses.)* ... you're making a mistake!
GEORGE. *(Dithers.)* Erm ...
ETHEL. I'll do it! *(She sweeps past MILDRED.)*
GEORGE. No, I'll do it.

(The both grip the handle of the bedroom door and push it open. They jam in the doorway as there comes the SCRAPE of a door key in the front door and HUMPHREY enters from the street. He's wearing a dark overcoat and a scarf over his pyjamas. He's got slippers on. He has a thick Sunday morning newspaper under his arm, complete with color supplement. He looks cheerful.)

HUMPHREY. By golly, it's a bit fresh out there this morning! Still, it'll be a nice day if ... Oh, morning, George, you're up, then ... *(GEORGE and ETHEL slowly turn, looking stunned.*) Morning, Mildred. (*Sees ETHEL. Looks surprised.*) Hullo, Ethel ...

ETHEL. (*Weakly.*) Humphrey?

GEORGE. I ... er ... I ... Where've you been?

HUMPHREY. Round the corner, to the news agents. I like to read the papers in bed on Sunday morning. (*Tosses papers onto the bed.*)

MILDRED. (*Comes down the stairs, justified martyr.*) Well, now ... (*To HUMPHREY.*) You'll never guess where Ethel and George thought you were ...

GEORGE. (*Hastily coming down stairs.*) Ah, no, no! I didn't ... no, not really. *She* may have done!

ETHEL. (*Also coming downstairs.*) Not at all ... no. *I* didn't ...

HUMPHREY. Didn't what?

GEORGE. Nothing! It's ... it's not important, Humphrey.

HUMPHREY. If you say so, George. (*A thought.*) Oh, the keys were in your coat pocket. I hope you didn't mind me borrowing it?

GEORGE. (*Anxious to please.*) No, no, no. Not at all ... pleasure.

HUMPHREY. Good. Well ... (*Sees suitcases.*) Are they *my* suitcases?

ETHEL. Yes. I ... I brought your clothes 'round.

HUMPHREY. I see ...

MILDRED. *(To ETHEL.)* So you want him to stay here, then? *(She smoothes her hair.)* He's more than welcome.

ETHEL. *(Looks from MILDRED to HUMPHREY, indecisive. Jealousy wins.)* I ... erm ... No! No, I don't! *(To Humphrey.)* Perhaps I ... I have been a little hasty ...

GEORGE. We all make mistakes, don't we, Mildred? Er ... why don't we have a nice cuppa tea? *I'll* make it ...

MILDRED. You certainly will. *(To ETHEL.)* And I'd like some toast, as well. Perhaps you'd make that?

ETHEL. Oh, yes, yes of course. I didn't mean to suggest that you and ... *(Dithers.)* Toast, yes ...

MILDRED. My P.G. Tips. And my Co-op sliced.

GEORGE. *(He and ETHEL head for the kitchen. To ETHEL.)* Trouble with you, you're a suspicious-minded old boot.

ETHEL. I don't have to take that from *you* ... *(They exit to the kitchen. HUMPHREY takes off the overcoat and hands it to MILDRED.)*

HUMPHREY. *(To MILDRED.)* They make a lovely couple, don't they?

MILDRED. Yes ... *(Indicates newspaper.)* Where did you get the newspaper?

HUMPHREY. I pinched it out of next door's letterbox ... *(Turns to reveal a rip in the seat of his pyjamas.)* ... and I ripped my pyjamas shinning down that bloody drainpipe!

(*MILDRED chuckles throatily, picks up the swearbox from the coffee table and rattles it at him playfully.*)

MILDRED. (*Chuckling.*) Swearbox! (*She pats his cheek and he joins in the chuckling.*)

CURTAIN

WHEN THE CAT'S AWAY 113

EPILOGUE

Line up. Applause. MILDRED steps forward.

MILDRED. Ladies and gentlemen ... First of all, I'd like to thank you for being such a marvellous audience. Both George and I would like to say that ... (*Realizes that GEORGE isn't beside her. Looks back at him. He's deep in though, fingering his ear.*) George? George?

GEORGE. (*Coming forward.*) Sorry ... sorry. What were you saying?

MILDRED. I was just telling the audience what we think of them.

GEORGE. (*Alarm.*) You can't do that, Mildred! They've *paid!* (*To audience.*) I do apologize for whatever it was she ...

MILDRED. I said they were *nice!*

GEORGE. Eh? Oh, yeah ... (*Grudgingly.*) They were all right.

MILDRED. Now *you* say something. Pleasant!

GEORGE. Pleasant?

MILDRED. Pleasant!

GEORGE. Yeah, yeah ... er ... I ... er ... (*Clears throat.*) Ah ... er ... it's always a great pleasure to visit (*Wrong town.*)

MILDRED. This is (*Right town.*)

GEORGE. I didn't say it wasn't. I just said it's always a great pleasure to visit (*Wrong town.*)

MILDRED. (*To audience.*) You must forgive George. He's not been feeling himself lately.

GEORGE. Yes, I have.

MILDRED. Or to put it another way, he ...

GEORGE. I *can* speak for myself, Mildred! In fact I have written out a little speech ... (*Rummages in pocket and produces a little slip of paper. Clears throat. Reads rapidly.*) 'Six bottles o' brown ale. Large can o' bitter. Three packets o' cheese an' onion ... (*Realizes.*) Oh. Wrong one. Well, what I wrote was something like ... er ... "I think you're smashin'. I can think of no greater thrill than performin' in front of you and ..." (*To MILDRED.*) I've had a thought.

MILDRED. Yes, George. No wonder the feller in the off license winked at you?

GEORGE. Yes.

MILDRED. Anyway ... Ladies and gentlemen, we'd both ...

GEORGE. Hang on. I've had *another* thought!

MILDRED. What?

GEORGE. (*Dawning suspicion.*) My overcoat ... the one Humphrey was wearin' in that last bit ... I keep it up in the wardrobe ... in our bedroom ... (*Indicates.*)

MILDRED. (*Slightly thrown.*) Ah, well ... Do you?

GEORGE. An another thing ... I heard that bit about him rippin' his pyjamas on the drainpipe ... How did *that* happen?

MILDRED. Well ... er ... (*Gay laugh.*) ... he was probably shinning up the drainpipe .. to get into our bedroom ... to get into the wardrobe ... to borrow your overcoat!

GEORGE. Oh, yeah ... yeah ... (*Chuckles.*) Oh, well, that clears that up, then.

MILDRED. Yes ... (*They both chuckle for a moment.*) Say good night, George.

GEORGE. Good night.

MILDRED. Good night.

(*A wave from all.*)

CURTAIN

WHEN THE CATS AWAY

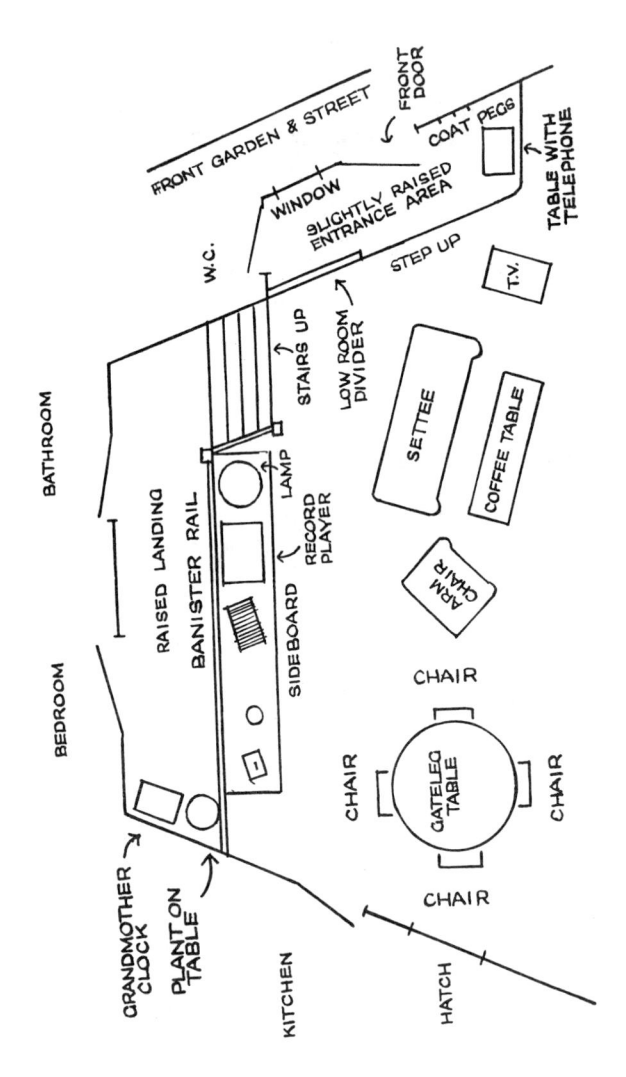

Picasso at the Lapin Agile
STEVE MARTIN

"Very good fun."
NEW YORK TIMES
"Very funny ... [and] daring."
NEW YORK POST

This long-running Off-Broadway hit places Albert Einstein and Pablo Picasso in a Parisian cafe in 1904, just before the renowned scientist transformed physics and the celebrated painter set the world afire. In his first stage comedy, the popular actor and screenwriter plays fast and loose with fact, fame and fortune as these two geniuses interact with infectious dizziness. 7 m., 2 f. (#18962)

Arts & Leisure
STEVE TESICH

Written by the popular author of TOUCHING BOTTOM, ON THE OPEN ROAD, THE SPEED OF DARKNESS and other plays, this brilliantly caustic play is centered around a self-absorbed drama critic who judges theater and life by the same criteria, to absurd extremes. He is confronted by the bitter and alienated women who have suffered from his unyieldingly clinical detachment and his habit of judging their suffering by its dramatic effect on him. 1 m., 4 f. (#3866)

Samuel French, Inc.
SERVING THE THEATRICAL COMMUNITY SINCE 1830

DEATH DEFYING ACTS
David Mamet • Elaine May • Woody Allen

"An elegant diversion."
N.Y. TIMES
"A wealth of laughter."
N.Y. NEWSDAY

This Off-Broadway hit features comedies by three masters of the genre. David Mamet's brilliant twenty-minute play INTERVIEW is a mystifying interrogation of a sleazy lawyer. In HOTLINE, a wildly funny forty-minute piece by Elaine May, a woman caller on a suicide hotline overwhelms a novice counselor. A psychiatrist has discovered that her husband is unfaithful in Woody Allen's hilarious hour-long second act, CENTRAL PARK WEST. 2 m., 3 f. (#6201)

MOON OVER BUFFALO
Ken Ludwig

"Hilarious ... comic invention,
running gags {and] ... absurdity."
N.Y. POST

A theatre in Buffalo in 1953 is the setting for this hilarious backstage farce by the author of LEND ME A TENOR. Carol Burnett and Philip Bosco starred on Broadway as married thespians to whom fate gives one more shot at stardom during a madcap matinee performance of PRIVATE LIVES - or is it CYRANO DE BERGERAC? 4 m., 4 f. (#17)

Samuel French, Inc.
SERVING THE THEATRICAL COMMUNITY SINCE 1830

✓✓✓✓✓✓✓✓✓✓✓✓✓✓✓✓✓✓✓✓✓✓✓✓✓✓✓✓

OTHER PUBLICATIONS FOR YOUR INTEREST

COASTAL DISTURBANCES
(Little Theatre- Comedy)

by TINA HOWE

3 male, 4 female

This new Broadway hit from the author of *PAINTING CHURCHES, MUSEUM,* and *THE ART OF DINING* is quite daring and experimental, in that it is *not* cynical or alienated about love and romance. This is an ensemble play about four generations of vacationers on a Massachusetts beach which focuses on a budding romance between a hunk of a lifeguard and a kooky young photographer. Structured as a series of vignettes taking place over the course of the summer, the play looks at love from all sides now. "A modern play about love that is, for once, actually about love--as opposed to sexual, social or marital politics . . . it generously illuminates the intimate landscape between men and women." --NY Times. "Enchanting."--New Yorker. #5755

APPROACHING ZANZIBAR
(Advanced Groups—Comedy)

by TINA HOWE

2 male, 4 female, 3 children --Various Ints. and Exts.

This new play by the author of *Painting Churches, Coastal Disturbances, Museum,* and *The Art of Dining* is about the cross-country journey of the Blossom family--Wallace and Charlotte and their two kids Turner and Pony--out west to visit Charlotte's aunt Olivia Childs in Taos, New Mexico. Aunt Olivia, a renowned environmental artist who creates enormous "sculptures" of hundreds of kites, is dying of cancer, and Charlotte wants to see her one last time. The family camps out along the way, having various adventures and meeting other relatives and strangers, until, eventually, they arrive in Taos, where Olivia is fading in and out of reality--or is she? Little Pony Blossom persuades the old lady to stand up and jump up and down on the bed, and we are left with final entrancing image of Aunt Olivia and Pony bouncing on the bed like a trampoline. Has a miracle occurred? "What pervades the shadow is Miss Howe's originality and purity of her dramatic imagination."--The New Yorker. #3140

Recent Hits From the "Master of Comedy" NEIL SIMON

PROPOSALS
LOST IN YONKERS

LAUGHTER ON THE 23RD FLOOR
JAKE'S WOMEN
RUMORS

BRIGHTON BEACH MEMOIRS
BILOXI BLUES
BROADWAY BOUND

LONDON SUITE
CALIFORNIA SUITE
PLAZA SUITE

Available in Acting Editions from
SAMUEL FRENCH, INC.